THE OTHER DOCTOR

And The Girl Who Ran Away

What do a Victorian Jewish detective, a thirteen year old girl, a vampire and William Shakespeare -the Bard of Avon - have in common? They're all acquaintances of the world's greatest time travelling wizard, Dr Thaddeus Bombay.

Join him on his adventures through "twistory" as he travels through time and goes in search of the truth behind the myths and legends of Wizard's Thatch, a small and insignificant town in Somerset that just happens to be home to the most magical school in the world: The Wizard's Thatch Academy.

The Other Doctor and The Girl Who Ran Away is the first in a series of page turning adventures that introduce you to the largest magical community in the world, the town of Wizard's Thatch where magic lurks on every corner.

It really is where magic begins....

Chapter 1

The two men stepped out of the telephone box. It was a bright red poppy colour and looked remarkably similar to the 1935 K6 traditional style telephone boxes that still pepper British streets.

There was no doubt that they were two of the most strangely dressed people she had ever seen. They were obviously in fancy dress, or actors in a play, or something. No-one normal dressed like that, did they?

"Hello, I'm the doctor." He said

Alice was startled to say the least. "Doctor who?" she stammered.

"No, that's the other fellow," said the Doctor a little impatiently, "and this is my friend Will." He said pointing to a younger man stood a little to his side.

"Hello," said Alice.

"Pleased to meet you," replied Will, holding out his hand. "Will Shakespeare at your service," and he bowed deeply.

Alice looked confused.

"Ssshh!" said the Doctor, "don't say a word – he doesn't know yet."

Will looked annoyed.

"He keeps saying things like that, but he never explains," complained Will. "He never tells you what he means, he just expects you to understand."

Alice looked from one to the other, even more confused than before.

"Err, I thought it would be blue," she said

Tired of explaining that the blue phone box in fact belonged to someone completely different, he just said, "No, it's red, as you can see."

"But you still have a phone box to travel in?" she asked, not quite believing what she was saying.

"No," he replied, "I was just making a phone call – Matilda is more of a mahogany colour……"

Alice was about to ask exactly who Matilda was and why she was looked like she was made out of wood but thought better of it as she gazed at the two strangers stood in front of her.

The man called the Doctor was quite tall, had a neat little beard and was wearing a pair of pin striped trousers, a white shirt with a gold brocade waistcoat and a deep red frock coat with a matching top hat. The hat looked like it might have been sat on though, as it was a bit squashed in the middle.

Will was much shorter; and although Alice couldn't quite believe it, was dressed almost completely in black, in traditional doublet and hose with flashes of white peeping through slashes in his sleeves and britches. He looked like he'd just stepped out of some great historical epic about Queen Elizabeth I. He was dressed like pictures she'd seen of the great Elizabethan playwright. He couldn't be *that* Will Shakespeare. Could he?

There was a pause.

"Now," said the Doctor, "You asked for help, so, here I am. What can I do for you?"

And that was how it started really. Alice took the Doctor by the hand and led him across the street to a tall and imposing Elizabethan building that looked as though it was sagging a little in the middle, almost making it look like it was grinning in a not particularly nice way.

"It's in there," she said

"What is?"

"It," she replied before bursting into uncontrollable floods of tears........

......

The hot sweet cup of tea had the desired calming effect.

They were sat at a small table in an old fashioned tearoom called Beattie's Victorian Pantry, a little further down the street from the building that Alice had pointed at. The warm and cosy atmosphere was beginning to relax Alice and calm her down. As her sobs gradually subsided, the Doctor was able to establish a few basic details: at some stage the previous night, Alice had apparently woken up to discover that she was being attacked by someone with a knife and had nearly fallen down the stairs in her efforts to get away. She had somehow managed to escape but was badly shaken. She had spent the rest of the night hiding.

"Quite understandable," said the Doctor.

Alice heaved a rather disconcerted and heavy sigh. "Let me tell you everything," she said.

… … … .

"Look at this," said Joe, Alice's father, "It's the most magnificent building and it's in our price range too!"

"Uhuh.." said Anna, her mother, who was obviously not paying any attention whatsoever and was leafing through a magazine looking for the horoscope.

"And it's in a charming little place called Wizard's Thatch."

"Where?" said her mother, rather disinterestedly.

"Wizard's Thatch," came the reply, "In Somerset," he said anticipating the next question.

"Never heard of it," said her mother, who was patently not interested as she started to read her horoscope.

"Show me! Show me!" cried Alice.

Alice was always impatient where her parents were concerned, as they hardly ever included her in decisions about the family's future – despite the fact that they had uprooted and moved twelve times in her life time so far.

This, if it were to happen again, would be the thirteenth home she had lived in – and she was only twelve!

Alice's father ran a small antique and curio business from where they lived, but the shop and house that they rented had been sold and they had to move in the near future.

He folded the newspaper to show details of a property that was to let and her mother got up to have a look.

"Listen to this," he said and began to read the advertisement out loud.

"Messrs Bombay and Bombay are pleased to offer this unique Elizabethan property on very flexible terms. Situated in the busy heart of the picturesque market town of Wizard's Thatch, the property benefits from an extensive retail space on the ground floor with surprisingly spacious living accommodation arranged over the upper floors and at the rear. There is a small rear courtyard garden and various outbuildings. Contact Bombay Manor Estates for details or to arrange a viewing. "

"Sounds lovely" said her mother, looking over Joe's shoulder at the advertisement

"Sounds creepy," said Alice.

"Look there's a telephone number. Why don't you call them Joe – we could go and have a look this weekend. I'll get a map to find out where exactly it is."

"Do we have to mum?" moaned Alice, who really didn't want to move again.

"It won't do any harm, will it?" said her father as he picked up the telephone and dialled the number in the advert. "And it's not like we've got a choice – the woman who owns the house we're in has sold it to a Somerset property company.

After just a few short rings the telephone was answered by a woman with a crystal clear and clipped voice.

"Good afternoon," said the refined voice, "Bombay Manor Estates, how can I help?"

"Hello," said her father. "My name is Joe Owens and I was calling about the property you're advertising in Wizard's Thatch."

"Aah, yes. There's been a considerable interest in it – we think we'll get an offer quite soon."

"Really? Gosh!" said her father. "We're the other side of Oxford, but we're really interested. Is there any chance that we could have a look inside this weekend?"

"Well, I'm not sure. We don't normally do weekend viewings. Could you come this evening? We close at half past five, could you be here by then?"

Her father put his hand over the receiver to speak to his wife and daughter.

"There's been a lot of interest already – let's go and have a look. But we'd need to leave straight away…" They both nodded, although Alice's nod was a little reluctant. Alice did not want to move again.

He spoke again to the woman at Bombay Manor Estates. "I'm not sure we can, is there any chance it could be a bit later?"

There was a short pause. "How much later?" she asked.

"About 7 ish?" said her father.

"Ordinarily I'd say no," Came the reply, "but you do sound genuinely interested. Will you be coming alone?"

"No," he replied, "I'd be bringing my wife and daughter with me, is that ok?"

"I see," there was another slight pause, almost as if she was conferring with someone else, "In that case, there will be no problem. I'll see you at 7 o'clock sharp. Do you know how to find the property?"

"Oh yes," said her father, "My wife, Anna, already has the map out. We're really interested – you won't accept any offers until we get there will you?"

"You have my word, Mr Owens," said the woman's voice on the other end of the phone.

"Until later then," said her father. "Goodbye"

"I think they'll be ideal," Valeria said as she placed the telephone handset back in the cradle of the old fashioned Bakelite telephone. Her long red finger nails tapped on the dusty antique mahogany desk.

She looked across the large book lined room at her brother who was sat in an old fashioned leather armchair beside a very ornate fireplace. The room really could do with a clean she thought.

Her brother did not reply.

Chapter 2

The car sped around the corner and screeched to a halt, the engine purring while it idled. The journey had taken her longer than she thought and the family were already waiting for her.

Valeria looked through the small windscreen of her very expensive black sports car at the family standing, huddled, outside the building that was to let. The rain had just started to come down and it was beginning to get misty. It was, after all, the beginning of October.

Long red nails gripped the top of the leather steering wheel before turning the engine off.

"Yes," she thought to herself, "they would do very nicely indeed."

She opened the car door and very elegantly got out. The 5 inch black heels of her shoes making her appear even taller than she actually was. She slammed the door shut and walked purposefully towards the building.

"Miss Bombay?" asked Alice's father.

"Mr Owens?" she asked in reply. "You found us easily enough then?"

Valeria Bombay studied the faces of Joe, Anna and Alice carefully. Alice felt very uncomfortable under the scrutinising gaze, but her parents didn't appear to notice.

"You must be Alice," she said.

"Yes, but how....."

"Let me show you around."

From out of nowhere she produced an old fashioned key ring with several large keys on it. They looked like jailers' keys thought Alice. Valeria selected one and placed it into the large keyhole on the door. As she turned the key Alice could have sworn she heard a far off scream.

Valeria looked at Alice sharply, and then said, "I see. Right, who wants to go first..?"

Alice and her parents walked through the door into a hallway with very old flagstones on the floor. The hallway seemed to go on forever with a large staircase rising from the centre and huge rooms to either side

"Oh, Joe," said her mother, "It's beautiful," her eyes shining with the possibilities. "Let's go and have a look at the shop area."

Beautiful was not a word that seemed appropriate to Alice at all. The shop was quite dark, with dark wooden panelling, dark red walls and a red carpet. It was also extremely dusty with cobwebs everywhere. And it smelt.... but what of? Damp, yes. Dust, certainly – but there was something else. It was almost a smell that you could taste, bitter and metallic somehow.

"Obviously it needs a small amount of work," said Valeria.

"Small!" Alice cried out before she could help herself.

"Nothing a lick of paint and a good clean wouldn't sort out," said her mother.

Alice looked at her mother incredulously – they obviously weren't seeing the same things! It was in a terrible state.

"What sort of business are you in?" asked Valeria.

"Oh, antiques, curios and old books," replied her father. "And this is ideal. It looks like it used to be a parlour or library or something."

"It's got loads of character, Joe. Unbelievably spacious and airy – you wouldn't have thought that the ceilings could be as high as they are from the outside would you? I love it," said her mother. "What do you think Alice?"

"*Oh I love it!*" she said rather sarcastically.

"Good, then it's settled" said her father. Then turning to Valeria he said "We'd like to make an offer."

Alice couldn't believe what she was hearing. They hadn't even looked at the rest of the building yet. She looked imploringly at her mother who looked as though she might be having doubts of her own.

"I think we should take a look at the rest of the building, Joe, just to be sure" she said. "But you're right, it is wonderful."

Valeria smiled – but it wasn't a nice smile thought Alice. It looked odd somehow. And, she thought, it looked hungry........

… ..

After a cursory glance around the building where her mother had cooed over the old fashioned plumbing and the size of the kitchen, her father reconfirmed his intention of making an offer by stating that they would pay the asking price.

"Marvellous," said Valeria. "I'll have the papers drawn up first thing in the morning."

Her father offered his hand to shake on it and Valeria drew back with a slight look of distaste crossing her features.

"Oh, there's no need to shake on it," she said recovering quickly. "You look eminently trustworthy."

Her father went a deep red colour – Alice had never seen her father blush before and it made her feel uncomfortable.

"I'll send the papers round as soon as they are ready – if there are no problems you could be in by the end of the month."

"What about references?" asked her mother.

"Oh, I don't think we'll need to worry about that, we're quite old fashioned and we go on trust a lot here," replied Valeria, ushering them back through the door. "Besides, I like the look of you."

She glanced around nervously. Something was obviously bothering her.

"Now, if there's nothing else, it's time to go," she said.

She locked the door behind them and Alice was certain that once again she heard a noise. This time, however, it sounded more like an ominous chuckle.

It was only as they were walking back to their car that she remembered something that Valeria had said: *"you could be in by the end of the month."* That would be Halloween. Alice began to feel like her world was closing in on her. How could this be happening so quickly?

Chapter 3

"Alice! Alice!" her mother called out to her daughter, "Are you packed yet? The removal lorry will be here soon."

"I hope not," muttered Alice as she slowly finished emptying her cupboards and put her most treasured possessions in a box clearly marked "Alice's Stuff". She really didn't want to leave this house and was trying to delay the final moment as long as possible.

"It's here, Alice!" Her mother sounded *very* stressed.

The large lorry pulled up outside the house with a squeal of breaks – the day that they were due to move had arrived and Alice had been dreading it. Ever since that day just a few weeks ago when they'd driven down to Wizard's Thatch, her world had been full of packing crates, suitcases and cardboard boxes.

"I hate moving," she thought, "although it would be great to stop living out of boxes again." Alice hated packing and although she was now very good at it (twelve moves in as many years) she still loathed it. Something always ended up where it shouldn't and you always managed to lose something precious. Last time they moved she'd lost her Grandmothers necklace, something she'd never confessed to.

The last four weeks since they'd seen the new house and shop in Wizard's Thatch had been a blur of telephone calls, goodbyes and packing. Her father had arranged for all of his stock from the shop to go into storage so it could follow shortly after they had moved in to the house.

There had been lots and lots of packing, and lots and lots of cardboard boxes. Alice thought that if she never saw another cardboard box it would be still be too soon!

While all of her friends were getting ready to go trick or treating and carving pumpkins, Alice had been packing. Her mother had assured her that they would still carve Jack O Lanterns when they got into the new house, but Alice was not so sure. Somehow the idea of spooky lanterns in the new house just filled her with dread.

The removal men worked hard and the furniture was soon loaded on to the lorry.

"Careful with that – it's an antique." Her father rushed across to where the two men were rather unsteadily carrying a rather large and extremely valuable carved wooden cabinet. It was very heavy and they looked like they were about to drop it.

"Drop it if you like," muttered Alice rather uncharitably.

It was a piece that she had never liked as it was rather ugly and was covered in carved wooden faces that seemed to be screaming out in agony. Every Halloween Alice avoided it because she was convinced that the faces would come alive and beg for help. It scared her.

Her father had once told her that it had a secret compartment but she'd never been able to find it. She had gone over every square inch one day – several times but to no avail, she simply couldn't find it.

It was a horrible piece of furniture and she shuddered just remembering all the times that she had woken up in the middle of the night convinced that she was hearing strange noises coming from the middle of the cabinet.

Finally they were ready to leave and the last piece of furniture and the last box had been loaded onto the back of the removal lorry. It was finally time to go. She took one last look at her bedroom and walked down the stairs and outside. She even wondered for a brief moment if she could stay in the house on her own, anything but move to the new house. For some reason the whole idea just filled her with dread.

"C'mon Alice – it's an adventure, think of all the fun we'll have getting the house ready for Christmas," her mother had said. Alice came to the realisation that her mother had never understood her and probably never would. She was growing up fast, *too fast* her mother always said. 'At least she got that right,' she thought.

Alice had a long and lasting look at the house they were leaving. They might have only been there for just under a year but it was the house that she had felt was most like home and she'd made friends faster here than anywhere else. She was really going to miss her friends, but her mum had said they could come and visit whenever they liked. But Alice knew it just wouldn't be the same. Whenever they moved her friends never came to visit – they always promised to but somehow there was always a reason why they couldn't. You'd think that Alice would be used to it by now, but she wasn't. It always hurt to leave friends behind.

"Come on Alice," said her father, "We'll stop off and buy some pumpkins on the way, if you like and we can carve them when we arrive."

"Oh great," was all she could manage. This was going to be the worst Halloween and birthday ever!

CHapter 4

Valeria Bombay was waiting for them as they pulled up outside the building in Wizard's Thatch. The sky was overcast and it was just beginning to rain.

"Welcome," she said, "to your new home. I know you will have some interesting times here, my brother and I did."

"I didn't know you and your brother used to live here," said Alice's father.

"Oh, we never lived here we just used to visit the people who did, but it was a very long time ago," she replied. "A different lifetime you might say."

"That's rather enigmatic."

Valeria smiled. "I'm an enigmatic woman, Mr Owens," she replied. "Well, here are the keys; I'll leave you to settle in. I won't come in though ~ I'll only be in the way."

"Thanks," said her father, "I can't believe how quickly we've been able to move in."

"Well, it is Halloween tomorrow and that's the end of our year, so we try to ensure that our properties aren't empty," there was a pause, "for financial reasons, obviously.…."

"And its Alice's birthday," said her mother, "so we need to be settled by tomorrow."

"Well, congratulations!" said Valeria, turning to Alice, with a smile that almost looked genuine. "How old will you be?"

"Thirteen," said Alice.

"Fascinating – where I come from thirteen was a very special birthday, a coming of age, you might say."

"I thought you were local?" asked Alice, "because you did say that you and your brother visited here, didn't you?"

"A long time ago, I was much…" there was a pause before Valeria continued, "…younger then." Valeria licked her lips and looked around. Nervously, Alice thought.

"Anyhow, it's nearly time for my dinner, so I'd better be off. Ta Ta!" And with that Valeria turned on her heel and was off.

"What a strange woman," said her mother

"But delightful," said her father with a slightly dreamlike quality to his voice.

"Just plain creepy," retorted Alice.

"That's unkind Alice," said her father in a reproving tone.

"True though," replied her mother. And she turned and smiled at her daughter. "Let's go and choose you a room before the removal lorry gets here."

But at that very moment the removal lorry careered around the corner and came to a screeching halt outside their new home.

"Don't you know how to drive?" her father demanded.

"Oh yes sir," came the gruff reply from within the lorry cab, "but it was the strangest thing – almost as if the truck couldn't wait to get here. 'Course, it's not our usual one, we had to borrow this one after ours broke down this morning. Still, we're here now – and' that's the main thing. Isn't it Arthur?"

It was at that point that Alice looked at what was painted on the side of the lorry for the first time. It was a bit grubby, but she could make out some letters and a few words painted in gold on the side of the lorry in old fashioned script. *B M E Removals*, it said.

"Excuse me," said Alice.

"Yes love," said Ted, the removal man.

"What does B M E stand for?" she asked.

"B M E? Why that's who we borrowed the truck off. Bombay Manor Estates they was called. Strange though," he continued. "We didn't call them, they just turned up at the depot this morning and said we might need some help."

"And they were right, Ted, weren't they?" said Arthur, his assistant.

"Still strange though," said Ted. "C'mon lad, lets start to unload."

"Right e o," came the reply. "'Ere, Ted, this place gives me the creeps. It look's like the building is grinning at us! And there's a kid peering out of the window on the top floor."

Alice began to panic – it really did look as though the building was grinning at her, and it wasn't a nice grin......
Just four weeks ago they had met Valeria Bombay for the first time and yet already the Bombay family appeared to be taking control of their lives...... And just who was it that was peering out of the top floor window as everyone in her family was still outside.......

CHaPTER 5

The clock had just struck seven times and the removal men had only just left. Alice was sure that more boxes had been unloaded than she had seen go on the removal van outside their old home – but that was impossible, wasn't it?

There were boxes everywhere; in the hall, on the stairs – even on top of the furniture. It almost looked as though the removal men had just dumped the boxes wherever they could, although at least they looked as though they were mostly in the right rooms.

"Thank goodness," said her mother, "I thought they were going to be here for ever."

"That's strange," Alice thought to herself," I thought they were in a hurry to leave. They unloaded faster than they loaded, I'm sure they did."

Alice was of course completely right. Ted and his assistant Arthur had been thoroughly spooked by the events of the day, and the journey to Wizard's Thatch had been, to use Ted's own words, "frankly terrifying!" They really couldn't wait to get away – so much so that they had almost dumped the furniture and boxes on the pavement. In fact, if her father hadn't kicked up a stink, they would never have set foot in the house at all!

Still, they had, after a bribe or two, taken everything inside and placed it in the rooms they were directed to. Undoubtedly it was in the wrong places, but it was at least all inside. Which was just as well, because the light rain that had started when they arrived had turned into a torrential down pour and it was quite obviously going to get a lot worse before it got any better.

Alice picked up her box of treasures, which she had insisted on carrying on her lap for the entire journey, and started to make her way up to the top floor where she had chosen her room. She had chosen a bedroom right at the top of the house overlooking the street. Although it was under the eaves with a sloping roof it was huge and would be the biggest bedroom Alice had ever had and there was another one next door for when friends came to stay.

As she trudged up the stairs she thought she could hear laughter coming from one of the rooms, but she knew that there was no-one there so just dismissed it as children running past the house outside in the rain. How she wished she was out there instead of inside – it was so gloomy here, and although she couldn't put her finger on it, she was sure that it felt wrong somehow. Like something terrible had happened here once.

She laughed nervously, as she glanced around. Her mother always said she had an over active imagination, and now Alice was beginning to think that she was right. It was just an old spooky house that was all.

Finally, Alice arrived in her room and looked around.

"What a mess," she thought.

She sat on her bed and put her box of treasures down beside her, before letting out a big sigh. It would soon seem like home once she got her own things around her.

There on the top of the box was an old family photograph that she had once rescued from the rubbish years ago when they moved. It showed her great grandfather when he was her age with his Uncle and Aunt shortly before they died. She tried to remember what it was that her father had said when she asked about them.

"It was a terrible tragedy," he had said. "They just vanished from their house in the country. No-one ever knew what had happened."

And that was it, she couldn't get any more of the story from him, or her grandparents who wouldn't talk about it at all.

"Now, shush!" her grandmother used to say. "Let's not disturb the past with daydreams and what might've beens. Best to leave well alone."

But that didn't stop Alice wondering what had happened. Perhaps they'd been kidnapped, or maybe they were smugglers or pirates. At least that was what she'd hoped while she was researching her family tree at her last school for a history project. But no matter how much she'd searched, and how many people she'd talked to there was nothing exciting about her family at all, no black sheep – not even a grey one! Her family, she had decided were the most boring family in the country. It didn't stop her dreaming though.

There was a light tap on her bedroom door. It was her father.

"Can I come in?" he asked. Alice nodded. "What's that you've got?"

"It's just that old photo," said Alice, "you know, the one with great aunt Anna and her husband in it."

Joe went very pale.

"I didn't know you'd still got that," he stammered. "I thought I'd thrown it away years ago."

"I saved it for a history project," she replied.

"Oh well, best put it away for now – you must be hungry."

Alice nodded.

"Come on then," said her father, as he lead them down to the kitchen at the back of the house where her mother was unpacking. "Let's celebrate our new home!"

When they walked through the door, Joe waved his hands airily around the room and said "Home, Sweet Home!"

"I think we'd better unpack a few things first," said her mother. "I have everything we need here." Producing a cool bag that she had packed earlier in the day, she unzipped it and brought out glasses, sandwiches and a bottle of old fashioned and very fiery ginger beer!

"Wow!" said Alice.

And they sat down amidst all the boxes and misarranged furniture for their first meal in their new kitchen.

"We'll have to rough it for tonight," said her mother, "but I'll soon have it all ship shape and Bristol fashion!"

"To the future!" they all toasted. The room was lit by a sudden flash of lightening throwing everything into stark relief. Shadows were cast into all of the corners making it seem as though there was something lurking that didn't quite belong.

There was a sudden loud crack of thunder and they were plunged into darkness as all the lights went out.

That was when Alice screamed.

Chapter 6

The Doctor put another cup of tea in front of Alice, and she looked up with tears in her eyes.

"It's ok," he said, "In your own time."

She smiled and picked up the cup, cradling it in her hands for a short while before taking a few sips. The tea was very hot and had a strange malty taste. She looked at the Doctor and he nodded encouragingly.

"Go on," he said, "It's good for you."

She took another sip and could feel the hot sweet tea warming her, coursing through her veins and filling her with the strength to continue her tale.

"What happened next?" asked Will.

"It was so awful," she replied, "I hardly know where to begin…"

The Doctor sat back and waited.

…

As the lightening had lit the room a face had appeared at the window, it was a long pointy almost haggard face and it was white, very, very white. But that wasn't really the problem. The really scary part had been when the face got very close to the window pane and then carried on coming – it just didn't stop!

Alice had screamed, her father, had got to his feet and her mother had cried out. And then it was gone.

"What on earth…" began her father.

"It's gone." Her mother sat down, still pale and still shaking. Alice was still looking at the window. "Come and sit down here," she said to her daughter.

But Alice remained where she was – you see, Alice had seen the message that was left on the window, the one that looked as though it had been written after you breathed on a window pane.

The one that said….

…. beware….

Chapter 7

Alice stretched. She was warm and comfortable under her duvet, and she could tell that the sun was shining through her bedroom window even though her eyes were still tightly shut.

"Maybe it was all a bad dream," she thought to herself. "Maybe we didn't move and we didn't spend the night in a strange, creepy old house. Maybe I didn't see anything in the window – but it was so real…."

She could hear her parents talking downstairs and the sound of a radio in the kitchen. She could also smell toast – at least she thought it was toast. It smelt like toast and it was all very reassuring.

"It must have been a dream," she thought.

Alice stretched again, luxuriating in the warm and safe feeling that was now spreading through her entire body, from the tips of her fingers to the tips of her toes.

That toast really did smell rather inviting, and she was very hungry. And it's my birthday she thought suddenly coming wide awake. She opened her eyes and came face to face with a strange bedroom full of unpacked boxes. It was all horribly true.

She stared around her room at the mispositioned furniture, the piles of cardboard boxes that contained all her worldly possessions and the suitcases full of clothes and shoes that were on the floor. Her earlier feelings of contentment came crashing down around her.

They had moved house, she had spent the night in a creepy old house and it was her birthday. But there were no presents. And she wouldn't be seeing any of her friends – they were all too far away.

This was going to be the worst birthday ever.

There was a tap on the door. It was her mother.

"Happy Birthday darling," she said, "Breakfast's ready downstairs."

…

When Alice got down to the kitchen, she found it was completely unpacked and tidy. "She must have been up for hours," Alice thought.

"Couldn't sleep, too much to do," said her mother, answering her unasked question. "And as I started unpacking there was a place for everything to go straight away – almost as if the kitchen knew what I'd got to unpack and provided the shelves that I needed!" She laughed to herself.

Alice sat down at the freshly scrubbed pine table to a mountain of toast. It was one of her favourite things for breakfast. She picked up a slice, liberally applying butter and pumpkin marmalade before taking a huge bite and taking stock of what she could see.

The Kitchen was huge. There was a flagstone floor, pale green walls and a huge fireplace that had an old fashioned range in it. Just off to the left there was a huge walk in larder with an old fashioned meat safe and ice box.

"I baked the bread this morning," said her mum, "because I wanted to try out the range and I knew that a freshly baked loaf would make us feel like it was really home."

And she was right, it had. Alice reached for another slice of toast and started to butter it. But she stopped with the butter on the knife halfway between the pat of butter and the toast. There on the table were two envelopes, one a brightly coloured one with Alice in what was unmistakably her mother's handwriting, and the other a stiff white envelope with her name written on it in an old fashioned scrawl.

"What's this?" she asked holding the second one up.

"It was on the doorstep when I came to call you," replied her mother. "I expect it's a birthday card."

"But no-one knows we live here."

"Oh, yes," said her mother distractedly as a saucepan started to boil over on the range. "I'll never get the hang of this old thing," she muttered under her breath. Then, to Alice, "Why don't you open it and see who it's from?"

Alice decided to open her mother's card first.

"Thanks mum," she said, "It's lovely."

"You'll get your present when your dad gets home, later."

It was only then that Alice noticed that he wasn't there. "Where's Dad?"

"Out," said her mother, "he's arranging for all the stock that's in storage where we used to live, to arrive – he wants to open the new shop on Saturday."

Alice turned her attention to the other envelope, the one with the old fashioned writing on it. She turned it over and there on the back was a heavy wax seal with the initial B in it. How curious.

She broke the seal and opened the envelope. Inside was an old fashioned correspondence card with Bombay Manor, Wizard's Thatch Halt printed across the top. The card held a hand written message. It said:

"Welcome to Wizard's Thatch. I wish you many things and an interesting birthday. Sincerely, Valeria Bombay."

"Who's it from," asked her mother.

"I.. it's from Valeria Bombay," stumbled Alice.

"That's nice," said her mother, clearly distracted.

But was it? Was it really nice, Alice didn't think so.

The sun went in briefly, plunging the kitchen into gloom.

Alice shuddered.

Chapter 8

Wizard's Thatch, it turned out, was quite a nice place to live – a bit odd perhaps, but nice never the less.

Once Alice had gotten over her fright of the night before ("Dodgy wiring," her Dad had said when he'd returned just after breakfast), she decided to leave the rest of the unpacking to her parents while she explored the town. "I'd only be in the way," she reasoned.

"Don't go far," her mother had called as Alice wound her way through the shop at the front of the house.

"As if," Alice thought. What a way to spend a birthday, there hadn't been any presents and no cards from her friends either. The streets around their new house were dark and narrow, but were stuffed with really interesting shops. Alice discovered the local supermarket called Witchrose, an old fashioned apothecary called Burke & Hare's (looks like a chemist, she thought) and an amazing sweet shop that seemed to sell every kind of sweet that you could possibly imagine.

Still, at least it wasn't raining or cold.

At that precise moment a large drop of water fell on her nose, rapidly followed by another and another, and then the heavens opened and it started to pour with rain.

Alice quickly looked for somewhere to shelter from the rain and ducked into a doorway to shelter. It was the entrance to a delightfully old fashioned looking book shop called *Tangled Words*.

The street lamp outside sputtered into life as the sky got darker and darker. There was a bright flash of lightening. Alice counted slowly: one, two, three, four and there was a low rumble of thunder. The storm was four miles away. Close enough to ensure she got soaked if she tried to get home.

She decided to stay exactly where she was and she hoped that the owner of the book shop wouldn't mind. She peered in trough the doorway and could see a man behind the counter leafing through a book that was resting on top of it. He looked friendly enough. As she was looking at him, he glanced up and smiled. Alice smiled back and he waved her in out of the rain.

"Hello," he said, with a friendly smile. "Are you looking for anything in particular.. or just getting out of the rain?"

"Just getting out of the rain," confessed Alice, "But I thought I might look around as well if that's ok?"

"Knock yourself out," came the reply. "The name's Jed, Jedediah Tangle, this is my shop – just shout out if you want anything."

"Thanks. We've just moved in down the road."

"Oh, you're the little girl that's moved into Alice's House – the old antique shop."

"But my name's Alice...."

"Strange coincidence that. But it's always been called Alice's House. Look, I'll show you." And with that he came out from behind the counter and reached into the window display.

"This," he said, "Is a History of Wizard's Thatch, and it's got a whole chapter about your house, look… "

Alice looked, and there it was, a whole chapter in the History of Wizard's Thatch called Alice's House. But when she looked a little closer she saw the rest of the title. It said, 'The Curious and Curiouser History of Alice's' House' and then in much smaller print underneath 'and its hauntings'.

"Is my house haunted, then?" asked Alice looking worried.

"No, it's just a legend. Look, there's nothing to worry about, no-one has ever seen anything there."

"But I thought the house had been empty before we moved in."

"Who told you that?" he asked.

"She did," said Alice pointing at the name on the cover of the book, "She showed us around the house a month ago."

"But that's impossible, "said Jed. "Valeria Bombay lived over 100 years ago…. "

Alice thought she was going to swoon.

Jed put out a steadying hand and led her to a chair.

"I didn't mean to worry you," he said. You probably met her grand-daughter. She's called Valeria as well and runs

Bombay Manor Estates. They own half the town you know."

Alice sighed in relief – it had been a simple misunderstanding.

"Look," he said, "Why don't you take the book and have a read – it's not a scary story and you can tell your family that it's a moving in gift."

"Oh I couldn't," said Alice, "No, really I couldn't."

"Well, consider it a birthday present then," said Jed.

"How did you know it was my birthday?" asked Alice.

"Oh! Err, I don't know – I meant an early present for your next birthday, whenever it is…." Jed now looked decidedly shifty and was trying to change the subject. "Look, the rain has stopped, best be getting home – wouldn't want Joe and Anna to worry, not on your first day."

Alice said thank you once again, and left holding the book tightly. It was only as she got half way home that she remembered that she hadn't told Jed what the names of her parents were either. She turned to go back and ask him, but all the lights in the bookshop were off and it said closed on a sign hanging in the window.

"How curious," Alice thought to herself.

She hurried back to the new house. As she went in through the front door, she saw her dad unpacking globes and astrolabes and putting them on the shelves behind the counter. The rest of the shop had antiques and curios everywhere. There were paintings on the wall, books on the shelves by the fireplace, a clock on the mantelpiece and furniture everywhere.

"What do you think, Alice?" he asked. "Looks almost as though the shelves were built for my stock, don't you think?"

Alice looked around the shop. It did indeed look like the shop had been designed for all her father's antiques and books. Everything looked like it belonged, almost as if it had always been there.

"Where did it all come from though Dad, I didn't know you had as much stock as this in the old shop?"

"I know honey, neither did I. But as they were unloading, it just kept coming – and I know that the van was empty when they started loading it at the lock up where it was stored. Who would have thought that all this could fit in a ford transit, eh?"

"How did you arrange it so quickly?" asked Alice.

"Miss Bombay sent some of her men round to help out – it was one of their vans that brought it all here actually. Wasn't that nice of her?"

She shuddered again, not for the first time that day.

"C'mon," said her Dad, "Let's go and have some lunch."

Alice wasn't sure she was hungry.

CHAPTER 9

The rest of the day had raced past. Her parents had bought her a beautiful pendant necklace as a birthday gift and given it to her just before she went to bed.

"It's very old," said her father.

"And very precious," said her mother, "so don't lose this one." Her father winked, so they did know about her Grandmother's necklace after all.

"And it's beautiful," said Alice.

"It's also quite unique – there isn't another like it anywhere in the world," said her father.

The necklace was silver and set with shiny black stones and sparkling white ones. Could they be diamonds Alice wondered? As if reading her mind, her father spoke.

"The black stones are polished jet from Whitby, and yes, the white ones are diamonds."

"But it must have cost a fortune!" cried Alice, "it's so beautiful." She literally was lost for words.

"I had some help with it," her father smiled. "And we thought it would end your birthday on a high."

"It certainly did! Thanks Mum! Thanks Dad!" Alice threw her arms round her parents and gave them a huge hug. This had turned out to be one of the best birthdays ever – despite everything.

Alice yawned – it had been a very long and tiring day and she was more than ready for bed.

"Night Mum, Night Dad."

"Night Alice," they both replied.

And with that, Alice went upstairs to bed still holding her most precious birthday gift ever. She'd got a few cards, been given some lovely presents and had made a new friend in the town's bookshop. And he'd given her a birthday present too.

As she got ready for bed, she saw Jed's present sitting on top of her dresser where she'd left it earlier. She thought she'd look up the history of her house before she went to sleep. Jed had said it was in there somewhere.

Alice opened the book and skimmed the first few pages til she came to the list of chapters. There it was…

'The Curious and Curiouser History of Alice's' House'
'and its hauntings'.

She got into bed, settled herself and then flipped through the pages til she got to the page she was looking for. Then she began to read…

One of Wizard's Thatch's most interesting buildings is the one known locally as Alice's House. No-one really knows where this name came from or how it stuck to the building that is otherwise and more properly known as 13 Regent Street.

Regent Street, in Wizard's Thatch, is full of interesting buildings but Alice's House is surely the most interesting of them all. Built in the early 1540's and expanded through the 17th and 18th centuries to become the building that we now love so much.

Originally built as a staging post and tavern in the 16th century, the building gradually became the largest coaching inn in the south west, easily surpassing all of its rivals, throughout the 17th and most of the 18th centuries. By the late 1700's however, the building had become a private house for members of the Bombay family who needed a town house in which to stay whilst conducting business in town. The property is still owned by them to this day, although they no longer live there.

Some speculate that the name Alice's House was first used by a little girl who saw the building and said it looked like the Cheshire Cat from Lewis Carroll's 'Alice in Wonderland', and there is no doubt that due to poor foundations and subsidence the building has settled in the middle giving it the appearance of a grin. But there is another, slightly more sinister theory linked to the building's history.

Sometime in the later years of Queen Victoria's reign, Joseph and Annalisa Bombay moved into the house shortly after their wedding. The house had been empty and unloved for some years and the young married couple breathed new life into the building. Of course, being a member of one of the wealthiest families in the country meant that money was no object and Joseph freely and lavishly spent on the property to make it a suitable family home for his young wife and their future children.

Joseph turned the whole of the ground floor into a library and parlour for himself where he could conduct business; he sold antiques and curios, while the rest of the Elizabethan property was beautifully restored. Sure enough, as soon as it was finished, Annalisa discovered that she was expecting their first child.

The whole town rejoiced, because Joseph and Annalisa were a friendly and likeable couple who went out of their way to help the locals (unlike most of the rest of the Bombay family!).

It was an uneasy pregnancy, and Annalisa suffered terribly becoming increasingly paranoid that the house was out to get her.

Joseph did his best to reassure his young wife, but everyone noticed that even he was beginning to be affected by the strains of his wife's pregnancy. He began to have a haunted look with large shadows under his eyes. He started to avoid the neighbours, and everyone thought it was just that he was having sleepless nights looking after his increasingly disturbed wife.

Then, on All Hallows Eve in 1887, Annalisa gave birth to a beautiful baby daughter, and they named her Alice.

It was like a spell had been lifted. The house that had seemed so gloomy for so long was now filled with laughter, and Alice's smile lit up every room she went into. Annalisa and Joseph went back to being the happy and devoted couple that they were before they were expecting. And Alice was loved by everyone that met her. They were so happy and content that people believed they were truly blessed.

Then one terrible night, a few weeks after Alice's 13th birthday, on New Year's Eve - during the worst thunderstorm anyone could remember ever happening in Wizard's Thatch - a piercing scream rent the town's streets. People woke from their slumbers convinced that they had had a nightmare. And then the scream came again, even more piercing than before.

The townspeople tumbled out of their beds and into the streets. "Where could the screams be coming from?" they wondered. And then they heard it again, for a third and final time. It was coming from number 13 Regent Street.

They hurried over and ponded on the door but there was no reply. The town's blacksmith, Quentin Decker, broke down the door and the townspeople rushed in.

The house was eerily silent. Quentin called out, but there was no reply - it was absolutely silent, almost preternaturally so. They searched the house, but it was completely empty, no one could be found anywhere at all. But that wasn't the strangest thing, for not only had Joseph, his wife and daughter vanished, but so had all of their belongings, books, furniture, clothes - even Alice's toys - everything had gone.

Except for one thing.

In Alice's bedroom, on the floor, was a long bladed knife and it was covered in blood.

Alice stopped reading.

"I wonder what happened to them?" she thought. "I wish I hadn't read it now, it's all a bit gruesome."

It was at that precise moment that the thought occurred to her that she might be in the very same room that the other Alice had slept in. And that there were an awful lot of similarities between the other Alice in the book and her.

"But it is only a story," she reminded herself.

Her father was called Joe, not Joseph; Anna could be short for Annalisa but it wasn't. Her mother had been called Anna after her great grandmother. And she, Alice, had just celebrated her 13th birthday – but they'd only just moved in. She hadn't been born there, nor had she lived there all her life – and she certainly didn't know all the neighbours.

No, it was just all a huge coincidence. "So don't be silly," she told herself.

And with that, she pulled the duvet over her head and closed her eyes.

Chapter 10

November 1st dawned as a bright and cheerful, crisp winter's morning. There had been quite a heavy frost overnight and that explained why Alice's nose was so cold.

She had completely forgotten about the story she had read just before she'd fallen to sleep the night before and was looking forward to the rest of her holiday before she started at her new school.

"I wonder what it'll be like," she thought to herself.

Wizard's Thatch Academy sounded very grand and the teachers all wore floor length robes in the school colours of green and purple. She'd seen pictures on the school website and it all looked very smart and terribly old fashioned.

"It's one of the best schools in the country," her father had said.

Still there was no point in worrying about it until she started and there was a whole town to explore before then! But first, breakfast – and something smelled really good!

Alice got out of bed, pulled on a dressing gown and headed downstairs.

When she got to the kitchen she couldn't believe her eyes – breakfast was going to be a magnificent affair. Her mother had cooked homemade potato waffles, that were piled high with scrambled egg and slices of crispy bacon, all topped with tomato ketchup. It was Alice's favourite breakfast and it was so good that she had seconds.

As she was about to leave the table, her mother had stopped her.

"Don't forget that we've got to go and get your new school uniform this morning."

Alice groaned. "Do we have to?" she whined.

"Yes we do."

Alice's heart sunk – how boring a morning was this going to be? She thought about all the school uniforms that had hardly had any wear and were all stored in a trunk upstairs somewhere. None of them had been worn for more than a term or two.

"What's the point?" Alice asked. "We won't be here very long, we never are. I'm never at a school long enough to get the use out of a uniform. Can't we just say they didn't have one that fit?"

"No we can't," said her mother in a firm voice. "We're going to go first thing and let that be an end to it." Then softening a bit she said, "but I did think we could have a girly morning afterwards and go shopping...?"

Alice perked up. "Could we have lunch out as well mum? In that little tearoom opposite?"

"Oh go on then," said her mother. "You didn't have much of a birthday, did you? So I thought I might make it up to you, how about that?"

Alice couldn't believe her luck – she loved shopping and it was a great excuse to explore the town. And if all she had to do was put up with a visit to the School outfitters, then what the heck? She could do that.

"Great!" said Alice, "Sounds brilliant! I'll just run upstairs and get dressed."

"Don't forget to brush your hair!" her mother called as Alice ran up the stairs to get ready.

...

Tatling and Twaddle, the school's outfitters, was just down the road from their new home. It was a huge half-timbered building that looked like a very old fashioned and traditional department store with brightly coloured and slightly out of place window displays that looked like they hadn't been changed in years and years. The store had four floors and a basement with a stone arch that marked the entrance to one of Wizard's Thatch's oldest streets: Magic Alley.

The huge windows had a yellow cellophane film stretched over them. "It's to stop the displays from fading in the sun," her father had once told her.

The main entrance looked a bit dirty and as they went through an old fashioned bell tinkled above their heads. After the brightness of the morning outside, both Alice and her mother had trouble adjusting to the gloom and found it hard to see. It was almost as if the sun was unable or unwilling to penetrate the gloomy and oppressive atmosphere inside the store. And where were the staff? The shop appeared to be deserted.

They closed the door and took a few steps further in. The gloom settled around them like a shroud, and they both shivered. To both sides were huge counters selling gloves and scarves – it all looked terribly old fashioned.

"Now where do we need to go?" her mother wondered.

"Look! There's a sign over there by the stairs," said Alice. "Academy Uniforms are in the basement."

"Let's go, maybe there's someone downstairs," said her mother.

Alice really didn't feel like going downstairs into the basement but she had no choice. The place was so gloomy and dark that it looked like it hadn't been cleaned in years. In fact that wasn't that far from the truth. She quickly pulled her hand away from the banisters as they were covered in a sticky dust.

"Eeeurgh!"

"Can I help you, madam?" came a deep and rather eerie voice from behind them.

Oh," said her mother, more than just a little flustered. "We've come to get my daughter a school uniform for the Academy."

"Aah, I see," said the owner of the voice, a tall and rather creepy looking man dressed in an old fashioned morning suit. "You must be Mrs Owens, and this must be Alice. This way please," he said as he brushed past," We've been expecting you."

And with that he headed down the stairs into the basement with Alice and her mother trailing behind him.

"How did you know what my name was?" Alice asked him.

"The school bursar rang and told us you were starting this term. We don't get many newcomers here."

"Oh I see," said her mother taking charge of the situation. "Come along Alice. Now I've got a list here somewhere of everything she needs."

"Don't worry, madam," said the man, in what Alice thought was a very threatening tone, "I know exactly what she needs."

...

Sometime later, after promises that the new uniform would be delivered the following day to the house, Alice and her mother set off for Beattie's Victorian Pantry – the tearoom just across the street.

"Thank goodness that's over," said her mother.

"You too?" cried Alice, "I thought it was just me?"

"It *was* rather gloomy," and then they both laughed. "Come on then, let's go for elevenses!"

...

Once they'd been shown to their table and perused the menu they'd ordered tea for two with extra crumpets as a treat.

The plate that arrived at their table was so full of toasted crumpets dripping with butter piled on top of each other that Alice though they would fall off the plate. They hadn't needed the extra ones – there were at least twelve crumpets on the plate and they were huge!

"Tuck in," said Beattie, the owner. At least Alice thought it was Beattie as she looked just like the picture on the menu. "I do like a girl with a healthy appetite." And with that she bustled off.

Despite it being only two hours or so since breakfast, Alice was famished.

"Steady on!" said her mother, after Alice had wolfed down the first crumpet in just three mouthfuls and had reached for her second.

"But they're wonderful," said Alice, "and they're much nicer when they're still hot!"

"Oh alright then, they are rather nice," said her mother as she reached for a second one herself. "What harm can it do?"

CHAPTER 11

The next few days passed in a blur, and all too soon the holiday was nearly over and Alice's first day at her new school loomed. Today was Friday and she'd soon have to face up to the prospect of making friends all over again.

Although she was used to starting new schools, it wasn't something she was particularly looking forward to. Every time was the same. She was always the new girl, always the odd one out, always the one that didn't belong.

Then, by the time she'd made friends and started to fit in, they always moved.

"It'll be different this time," said her father, "You'll see. We're going to put roots down here, I know we are. It feels," he paused, "different, it feels right somehow."

Alice thought that it felt anything but right.

There was something odd about this town, but she couldn't quite put her finger on it. True, the house they were living in was a bit strange, but she'd got used to that already. The townspeople were all terribly polite, and almost old fashioned she had thought, but she'd got used to that as well. She'd even got used to her new school uniform and that was really odd – she hated uniforms!

But there was still "something"... she just couldn't quite put her finger on it.

...

That night she went to bed thinking about her first day at her new school which was now only two days away. To try and put it out of her mind, she picked up the present she'd been given by Jedediah Tangle, the bookshop owner. *"A History of Wizard's Thatch"*.

Alice hadn't looked at it since the night of her birthday and she started to leaf through it. There seemed to be a lot of interesting stories about the town and its history, but none of them caught her eye, so she closed the book and was about to put it down when she gasped out loud.

It was the first time she'd looked properly at the picture on the back cover, the author's picture. It was a picture of the same woman who'd shown them around the house before they moved in; the woman who'd sent her a birthday card; the woman who creeped Alice out whenever she saw her; the woman who Jedediah Tangle had insisted was the granddaughter of the woman who wrote the book. But it was the same woman – they were identical, absolutely identical.

Alice almost dropped the book. How could that be? But wait…. There was something else…

She shot out of bed and grabbed hold of the necklace that she had been given for her birthday by her parents. She held the necklace in one hand and the book in the other looking first at one, then at the other.

Valeria Bombay was wearing the same necklace in the picture on the book. There couldn't be two surely? It must be the same necklace. Hadn't her father said that it was unique? And valuable? In fact, hadn't he said that he'd been given some help getting hold of it as well?

Alice pulled on her dressing gown and ran downstairs.

"Dad?" she called out.

"In here love," came the reply. He was obviously still in the shop fussing around getting it ready for the Grand Opening the following morning.

"Dad? About the necklace," began Alice.

"I know it was extravagant, but you're well worth it."

"But can we afford it?"

"Well.... I suppose yes is the answer, because it didn't actually cost very much," replied her father a little sheepishly.

"But you said it was valuable."

"Oh, it is. No really. It's worth a small fortune."

"Then, how... "

But before she could finish, he started to explain. "I should have told you before. It was sort of a gift."

Alice couldn't believe her ears.

"What do you mean, sort of a gift?" asked Alice, "and from who?"

"Look, I promised not to say anything," said her father, "but your mother and I agreed that we'd tell you if you asked. It was a moving in gift for you from Valeria – but she thought you wouldn't accept it if you knew it was from her, so she told me to tell you it was from your mother and me."

"Mum knows?" asked Alice, a note of incredulity entering her voice.

"Yes," replied her father. "She agreed with me that we'd be totally honest if you actually asked, but otherwise we wouldn't say a word. Your mother was of the opinion that it was too much for a gift from someone we hardly know."

"But dad," said Alice, "why did you accept something so valuable?"

"I know honey, but Valeria told us that she'd been given it for her thirteenth birthday and as she hasn't got any children of her own to pass it on to, she thought she'd pass it on to someone who'd appreciate it. You do like it don't you?"

Alice just didn't know what to say.

Chapter 12

Saturday morning dawned another cold crisp and beautiful winter's day. The sky was an icy blue and there was definitely a nip in the air. Once again Jack Frost has been through Wizard's Thatch overnight leaving his delicate lacy patterns on all the windows and pavements and a blanket of sparkling frost all over the ground. All of the trees looked like they were sparkling with diamonds. It was a perfect winter's morning.

Valeria Bombay sat in the driver's seat of her car, tapping her long red finger nails against the steering wheel. She's been waiting for this day longer than she cared to remember – it felt like a lifetime of waiting. For most people it probably was.

She stared at the house. No-one was stirring, it was too early, and she had placed the box on the doorstep where it couldn't fail to be noticed. Everything was in place. Joe's antique and curio shop was due to open this morning; his family were living in the house above it; Alice had celebrated her 13th birthday there just a few days ago and she had the necklace.

Valeria's hands gripped the steering wheel very tightly for just a moment and then she relaxed, her long red nails looking almost like talons as she considered everything that had happened over the last few weeks: the advert; the interview; the damaged removal lorry – everything – even down to the carefully placed lots at auctions making sure that the right person bought what she was selling. It had been so much to organise in such a short period of time.

Valeria was tired, and she felt old but at least she didn't look it she reminded herself – and if everything went to plan it would soon be over.

Everything was exactly as it should be; she started the engine, put the car into gear and sped off.

What could possibly go wrong?

CHAPTER 13

The opening of the shop was going to be a huge success. Her mother and father had worked ever so hard planning everything down to the last detail; they'd even invited a special guest to cut the ribbon at eleven.

There were glasses of wine for the customers, homemade cheese straws that Alice and her mother had been baking since early that morning and everything was sparkling clean.

A crowd had begun to gather outside, the sky had stayed clear and the sun was shining bathing in the shop in a warm golden glow.

"The sun always shines on the righteous," said Bob Black, the ironmonger.

"Indeed it does," agreed his partner Quentin Decker, "indeed it does."

Inside the shop, her father was beginning to get flustered. He'd been up since the early hours getting everything just so, just perfect. This was his dream. Since he was a young man he had always wanted a shop that looked as warm and inviting as a Victorian parlour and library but where everything was for sale and he had finally achieved it here in Wizard's Thatch.

He could've sworn he'd seen Victoria Bombay's sleek and expensive sports car parked in the street outside when he looked through the window first thing that morning, but by the time he'd gotten downstairs and opened the door the car had gone. He must have been mistaken.

Almost as if she'd been keeping an eye on the place making sure nothing went wrong for him, he thought. But then he dismissed the thought as he saw what was on the doorstep: a case of wine and a beautiful black handled paperknife.

"*Compliments of Bombay Manor Estate*" said the card.

How nice, he thought. And then he'd begun to panic. He hadn't thought about wine, what else had he forgotten? But that was all much earlier in the day. Everything was now in place, everything was perfect. All he needed was his guest of honour to turn up so they could open the doors. He looked nervously at his wife.

"Five to eleven," she said coming up behind him and making him jump just a little. "I hope she's not late."

"She won't be," he said confidently.

"Who, Dad? Who won't be late?" asked Alice

"It's a surprise, but I do hope she remembers," said her mother.

At that precise moment, the crowd outside stopped talking and almost as one turned to allow a very expensive looking black sports car to pull up outside.

The car looked familiar, Alice thought; maybe she'd seen it around town.

"I wonder who it belongs to," she asked herself.

The car pulled to a stop, and then, just as the clock began to strike the hour, the driver's door opened, and Alice saw a long and elegant leg appear with a black shoe with a 5 inch heel appear. This was quickly followed by another leg and then the rest of the body that it was attached to. They belonged to the last person that Alice wanted to see: Valeria Bombay.

The crowd were hushed, almost reverential as she carefully closed the car door and adjusted the extremely wide brim of her obviously very expensive black hat. Her father rushed out.

"M.. M.. Miss Bombay," he stuttered, "So glad you could make it." Her father looked bright pink with embarrassment.

"I wouldn't miss this for the world," she replied.

"I couldn't find any scissors, for you to cut the ribbon," said her father. The crowd chuckled good naturedly, "So I thought you could use this..."

There was an audible gasp from the crowd as he produced a long bladed black handled knife, the same one that had been left with the wine that morning. The blade glinted in the morning sun.

"This will do perfectly," said Valeria grasping the handle of the knife.

She strode purposefully toward the doors where Alice was waiting with the knife gripped firmly in her hand and raising it high above her head with one quick and really fast slash cut the ribbon that Alice was holding in front of her.

"I declare the Wizard's Thatch Curiosity Shop open for business," she declared.

Everyone breathed a sigh of relief and then clapped politely. Then, after waiting for Valeria to be invited over the threshold into the shop as the first customer, her father invited everyone in to have a look around.

Her mother was beaming and was handing out glasses of wine and offering her cheese straws to everyone.

"Where did the wine come from?" asked Alice, knowing full well that her father hadn't had time to organise that for himself.

"It was on the doorstep when I got up," said her father vaguely.

"You mean someone just left it without saying who it was from?"

"Not exactly," he replied, "there was a card."

"Well what did it say?" asked Alice.

"With the compliments of Bombay Manor Estates," interrupted her mother, "It was very generous considering everything else they've done to help us move in."

"Everything else?" asked Alice quietly.

"Yes dear," said her mother, "without Valeria's help we would never have got in before your birthday, and she seemed to think it would be better if we were already in so that you could celebrate it in your new home."

Anna thrust a plate of her homemade cheese straws at Alice who had gone rather pale. "Now stop asking questions and hand round these cheese straws." She added.

"Are you okay love?" asked her father who had just wandered over.

"Why didn't you use scissors to cut the ribbon, dad?" asked Alice.

"Do you know, it's the strangest thing," said her father, "but when I looked this morning I couldn't find a pair of scissors anywhere in the house."

"I know," said her mother with a faraway look, "not even in the kitchen. But do you know, as soon as the ribbon was cut, I opened a drawer for the corkscrew so that I could open the wine and there they were. Every single pair – in the same drawer."

"And where did the knife come from?" asked Alice in a small voice.

"It was with the wine," replied her father moving off to talk to some of their neighbours who looked like they were going to be his first customers.

Another gift from Valeria Bombay. Another strange coincidence. It was all too much, and with that Alice promptly fainted.

...

When Alice came to, she was tucked up in bed and her clock said it was early half past four. It was nearly dark outside.

She got up and looked at herself in the mirror. "Peaky" she thought to herself, and went downstairs.

"Are you feeling a bit better?" asked her mother.

"Yes thanks. What happened?" She asked.

"Well," began her mother, "when you passed out everyone was concerned and crowded round but that nice doctor from down the road was here and he soon shooed everyone away to give you some space."

"Then one of the men from the chemists helped me carry you upstairs," continued her father, "Mr Hare, I think his name was."

"Great," thought Alice to herself, "what an embarrassment."

"He really is rather nice that Dr Jekyll," mused her mum, "and he told me not to worry as you were probably just over tired. Mr Hare popped by with a herbal tonic for you to take before bedtime. He says he swears by it. Guarantees you a deep and uninterrupted sleep he says."

"Everyone was really concerned," continued her father, "even that Jedediah Tangle from the bookshop. He's a lovely fellow, says he's got some old books that he can let me have. Thinks they'd be more at home here than in his cellar."

"I'm so sorry," said Alice quietly.

"Whatever for?" asked her father.

"For ruining your big day…" she mumbled.

"Don't be silly – it's been a great success!" he replied. "In all the years we've had this business, and in all the different towns and shops we've never had it so busy. It's almost like everyone in the town was making us feel at home or something."

"Like we belonged here…." Said Alice

"We do belong here," said her father. "This was the best move we ever made. Don't you think so?"

Alice wasn't so sure.

"Anyway, we're closed now so we can put our feet up for the rest of the day and I'm exhausted," he said.

"You do look tired, Dad, didn't you sleep well last night?"

"No, hardly at all – and I was up ever so early. I was really worried about today but it was a great success, so I don't know why I was so worried really."

"But if you hadn't worried you would have been in a terrible state," said her mother, "And if it hadn't been for Valeria it still might have been! I mean, fancy forgetting to buy wine for the opening!" Her mother laughed, and then so did her father.

It had been a very long and stressful week, but it was all over now. Alice suddenly realised that she was really, really hungry. They'd been so busy that she hadn't really eaten any breakfast – and she'd missed lunch.

"When's dinner, mum?" she asked.

"You know I haven't even thought about it," her mother replied.

"Well, we've had such a successful day, why don't we eat out to celebrate?" said her father. "What do you think Alice?"

"Was it really a good day?" she asked.

"An absolutely brilliant day," he replied. "I'll have to get more stock to sell if this keeps up of course – although that Mr Burke from the chemists said that he's got a lot of things that I might be interested in."

"I thought you said his name was Mr Hare?" asked Alice.

"No, that's the other chemist – there's two of them, been in the family for generations apparently. Anyway, this Mr Burke says that they keep inheriting antiques and curios from their elderly customers when they, you know, pass on."

Alice stopped what she was doing. "Pass on?" she asked.

"You know… die," said her mother.

"Ohhh!" said Alice slowly as recognition dawned.

"Anyway, what about dinner?" her mother asked.

"Why don't we eat at the Golden Broomstick in the Square? It looks lovely in there," said her father, "and I'm sure there'll be something on the menu that we'll all love!"

So with the plans made, her mother and father set about tidying up with Alice's help and soon enough they were ready to go out.

Chapter 14

Alice could not believe how hungry she was, but at least dinner wouldn't be long she thought. The decision to eat here was a really good one as she liked the look of just about everything on the menu – but had settled for the "Golden Broomstick Special" as had both her parents.

While they were waiting for their dinner to arrive they looked around at the slightly odd interior of the tavern. It looked very old indeed and was spotlessly clean, but it felt, well, a bit odd Alice thought. She couldn't quite put her finger on it, but something wasn't quite right.

"This is lovely, isn't it," said her mother.

"Not very busy, though, is it?" said her father. "I hope that's not a sign!"

There were cobwebs in the chandeliers and in the corners – but it was just after Halloween she reasoned so they probably weren't real, and the straw on the floor was obviously meant to be there – but there was something. She didn't know what it was, but there was definitely something, and no matter what anyone else thought – she was certain that they were being watched.

However, all these thoughts disappeared as soon as the food arrived.

Alice could not believe her eyes – she had never seen such an enormous portion of food in her life.

First there was the burger, it was huge, must have been at least a half pounder on a wholemeal bun that was obviously homemade. Then there were the toppings: three different cheeses, pickles, lettuce and tomato all topped with crispy onion rings and a great big dollop of "special sauce" whatever that was. And then there was the bowl of fries smothered in cheese that was on the side – it was big enough to feed a family, and they'd ordered it three times!

They all looked at each other and laughed – all the strains of the day just melting away like the cheese was doing all over the fries. Fantastic!

"Back to normal, then?" laughed her father.

"Oh yes!" said Alice as she started the monumental task of clearing her plate.

No-one said much at all whilst they were eating as there was just too much food, but they all managed to clear their plates completely.

"Wow!" said Alice, "I'm stuffed!"

The waiter who had come to clear the table laughed and said "You won't be wanting the desert that's included with the special then?"

"Oh I don't know," said her father, winking at Alice, "I'm sure we could give it a try!"

"Ok," said the waiter with a smile, "Be right back then."

Sure enough, within just a few minutes he was back with three of the largest ice cream sundaes Alice had ever seen.

"They're a house special," he said, "They're called God Save The Queen!"

The sundaes were huge in tall ice cream glasses with long spoons. Each was filled with three flavours of ice cream: a luscious red strawberry, local creamy vanilla and blue bubblegum flavour. Smothered in strawberry syrup, whipped cream and with a glace cherry on top.

"Yum!" thought Alice.

Despite declaring that she was full to bursting, Alice managed to eat the whole sundae and licked her lips with pleasure when she finally put down her spoon.

"Now I really am full," she said.

"Me too," said her father, "Couldn't eat another mouthful!"

"I'm not surprised," said her mother gazing fondly at them both, "I've never known either of you eat so much!"

"Well, we all missed lunch," said her father.

"And I haven't been well," added Alice.

They all laughed.

Joe signalled the waiter for the bill so that he could pay and they could all go home, put their feet up and finally relax.

"Was everything alright with your meal, sir?" asked the waiter.

"It was… incredible," said her father. "Just the bill, please."

"It's taken care of sir," replied the waiter. "It's on the house – welcome to Wizard's Thatch!"

They all beamed at the waiter.

"Are you sure?" asked Anna.

"Absolutely," said the waiter, "On the express instructions of the management!"

"Oh, thank you ever so much," said her mother.

"A perfect end to a perfect day," added her father. "It's been such a long day and that was exactly what we needed."

Alice just sat back and sighed contentedly.

"How lovely," said her mother looking at the waiter. "Makes me feel like we really belong."

"Come on you two," said her father. "Before they change their mind. Let's make a run for it!"

They all laughed again as they put their coats on and prepared to leave. But as they did, Alice once again got the feeling that they were being watched. She looked around but could see no-one looking in their direction. She must be mistaken. She shrugged her shoulders and followed her parents out of the door.

The waiter, who had returned to the bar on the opposite side of the tavern to where Alice and her family had been sitting, placed another glass of what looked like thick blood red tomato juice in front of a customer who, as Alice correctly felt, had been watching them throughout the entire meal.

Her long red talon like fingernails tapped the glass as she gripped it and raised it to her lips for a sip and she smiled.

'It really was going perfectly to plan', she thought to herself, as she watched Alice and her family leave.

Chapter 15

Having slept most of the day away, Alice wasn't in the least bit tired and didn't want to go to bed.

"Well, it's not like it's a school night is it?" said her father. "So, I suppose you can stay up late tonight if you like."

"Thanks, dad!" said Alice, flicking through the tv listings. "Look, there's a horror film on tv, can we watch it?"

"I'm not sure, Alice," said her mother. "As long as you don't get nightmares."

"Mu-u-u-u-m!" cried Alice indignantly, "I'm not a baby anymore – I'm thirteen!"

"And a typical teenager already!" said her father under his breath.

They switched on the tv and surfed through the channels until they found the horror film – a classic black and white horror film called The House On The Hill, about an empty house haunted by dispossessed spirits. They settled down to watch the film with a mug of cocoa.

...

It was nearly midnight when the film ended, and by then Alice was nearly asleep – the cocoa having done its job. She was obviously a lot more tired than she had thought.

"Time for bed, sleepyhead," said her father.

"You could be right," yawned Alice. "Night mum, night dad!" and off to bed she went.

Tomorrow was only a few minutes away and tomorrow was Sunday – her last day of freedom before starting at her new school. What was that saying her mother used to use... oh yes.... Tomorrow never comes.

Well, it would soon enough.

Alice got into bed and closed her eyes. She was asleep before her head even hit the pillow. The digital clock on her bedside table said 23:47, it was thirteen minutes to the witching hour, but Alice didn't know what the time was as she was already dreaming.

Little could she know exactly what tomorrow would actually bring?

...

Alice's eyes struggled open. "What was that noise?" she wondered. Her eyes focussed on the clock and she groaned.

05:15, it said.

Alice groaned to herself. She'd probably dreamt the noise and it was ridiculously early, far too early to wake up – and she hadn't been asleep very long at all. She closed her eyes and quickly began to drift off once more.

Then she heard it again.

Her eyes snapped open this time. It sounded like a footstep on a creaky floorboard in her room. But it couldn't be, could it? She was imagining it surely. She really shouldn't have watched that horror film, her mother had been right after all.

She closed her eyes, but wait.… there it was again.

Alice held her breath. Whoever it was, was in her bedroom and was just the other side of her bed right behind her.

There it was again. Another footstep.

Alice tried to make out the shadows opposite her on the wall in the moonlight. Was that someone moving?

Yes! It was!

It was a man and he was holding what looked like a long knife in his hand, and he was trying to quietly creep towards her.

Alice screamed and leaped out of bed – there on the other side of the room was her father with a completely evil grin on his face and he was holding the knife that had been used earlier to cut the ribbon when the shop opened.

And it looked like it was dripping with blood!

Alice screamed again and ran out of the room and down the stairs towards the shop where she could hide.

"Help! Help!" she cried. "Someone, anyone! Please help!" But of course there was no-one there to turn to. And whose was the blood on the knife?

Alice was terrified. Her mother hadn't answered when she'd called out for help and the front door was locked. But even if it hadn't been where could she have gone? She didn't really know anyone in the town and those she did know she didn't trust.

Alice crept behind the really big ugly cabinet that she had never liked, thankful for the first time that it was big enough to hide behind. She started to cry, silently.

...

She stayed hidden for the rest of the night, and then when it was beginning to get light she crept out of her hiding place. She picked up an old cricket bat from the shop in case she needed to protect herself and crept carefully back up the stairs.

She paused outside her parents' room. The door was open, and she peered inside. Joe and Anna appeared to be fast asleep in bed – in fact they were both snoring. Everything looked completely normal. Had she dreamed everything last night? Had it really been a nightmare after all?

Still unsure, she crept up the stairs to the top floor to her bedroom in order to get dressed. And there, in the middle of her bed, was Jed's book with the knife stuck right through the middle of it.

Alice stifled a scream, hurriedly got dressed and then silently crept down the stairs to the kitchen. She got the spare keys that were hanging by the fireplace and left the building.

What on earth was she going to do?

Chapter 16

"And that's what happened," said Alice sniffling and taking another gulp of tea.

"Interesting," said the Doctor glancing at his companion Will. "Very, very interesting....."

Will, who had been taking notes whilst the Doctor listened carefully to everything that Alice had to say, put down his pen. It wasn't a normal pen, but a large feather quill that he had had to keep dipping in a pot of ink while he made his notes on sheets of parchment.

"What do you think, Doctor B?" he asked.

"Doctor B?" asked Alice, "What does the B stand for?"

"Why, Bombay of course," replied Will before the Doctor could stop him.

Alice shrank back away from him looking frankly terrified.

"You... You're a Bombay?" she cried.

"Oh don't worry," said Will quickly, trying to repair the damage his thoughtless statement had caused, "He's not like some of the other members of his family at all. Well, except for his younger brother Joseph, he was alright."

"Joseph?" asked Alice quietly.

That's right," said the Doctor. "Joseph was my brother, and Alice was my niece."

"Was?" Alice was almost too afraid to hear the answer.

"We don't know what happened to them. They just disappeared – my whole family did."

"All the living ones, anyway," muttered Will under his breath.

"Wh... What?" stammered Alice.

"Let me explain," said the Doctor. "It all started a very, very long time ago with the creation of the Rules Britannia... ."

Will took up the story and explained:

"Let's start at the very beginning, the Rules Britannia is not, as some people think, a jolly old song to sing along to, oh no. The Rules Britannia is a book of incredibly powerful spells and enchantments created by one of the most powerful wizards that the world has ever known. His name was Bran the Blessed, and he was born in the eleventh century making him incredibly and unbelievably old.

The Rules were created to protect the borders of what was to become the United Kingdom of Great Britain from invasion by marauding infidels and were quite successful for nearly nine centuries.

Their origins are considerably older.

In the first century AD (the year 61AD to be precise) Boudicca, was crowned Enchantress of the Isles (all 6,000 of them – that's right there are about 6,000 separate islands that make up what is known as the British Isles and they amount to a total land area of approximately 121,674 square miles) and she decreed that to keep her kingdom safe, a great magic would need to be wrought.

It took just over 100 years for the great spell to be prepared with a talisman planted on each and every one of the islands. Then in 1066, after the great battle between the Dark Wizard Galangal and Bran the Blessed, the Rules Britannia were finally and irrevocably invoked sealing the British Isles from invaders.

In 1877, Her Imperial Majesty Queen Victoria, Enchantress of the Isles and the Colonies, instructed the greatest wizards of her empire to strengthen the Rules Britannia with enchantments from the Far East. After much debate, the decision was made to enact a new enchantment; a codicil to the original Rules Britannia if you will, that would need to be renewed at the turn of the nineteenth century and then every hundred years thereafter on New Year's Eve.

Through the latter part of the nineteenth century all the preparations were put in place for the most powerful spell casting in history. As the time approached for the enchantment to be cast, the most powerful wizards and witches of the British Isles, The Council of Twelve, gathered together in the Great Hall of Bombay Manor in Wizard's Thatch: one for each of the twelve great Wizarding families.

But something went wrong. Terribly wrong.

The gathering started the chanting of the codicil at eleven o'clock at night – the whole enchantment was due to finish at the stroke of midnight, but as the clock was about to strike for the twelfth time three white mice ran across the Great Hall and through the circle of witches and wizards, causing Artemisia Bombay, who was terrified of mice, to lose her concentration. She screamed and let go of the hands of the wizard on either side of her as she picked up her skirts and stepped backwards out of the circle and out of the ring of magical protection that had being created.

There was a loud clap of thunder as the clock struck twelve and she promptly disappeared, as did every other living member of the Bombay family who was alive at that moment in time.

The rest of the assembled company quickly finished the codicil and tried to search through time for Artemisia and the rest of her family but to no avail. They had all vanished completely without a trace of their whereabouts being left behind.

Apart from those in the Great Hall, Bombay Manor was silent. Empty. Everything that the family had been doing as the stroke of midnight fell was still there, exactly where it had been dropped as they disappeared.

Beds had indentations where the younger family members had been sleeping; rocking chairs were still rocking; books were still open to the page that was being read when those holding them had disappeared; and the kitchens still had a fire lit with a whole hog roasting over the flames on a spit – now slowly burning as there was no-one left to turn it as all the family servants had also disappeared. But that wasn't the only magic wrought that night.

A terrible curse had also fallen on the inhabitants of Wizard's Thatch - all 8,786 of them – but no-one would talk about it. It was a complete mystery.

The only living member of the Bombay family to survive this tragedy was Dr Thaddeus Bombay who was "away" at the time travelling with me. When we returned, he was as mystified as everyone else – but perhaps the worst thing for him was that he believed it to be his fault. Artemisia (his younger sister) had taken his place at the gathering and if she had not been there she would not have broken the circle."

"So how did you survive?" asked Alice.

"We were travelling," said Will, simply, "So we weren't *actually* alive at the time the spell went wrong."

Alice looked horrified.

"He doesn't mean we weren't actually alive," explained the Doctor quickly. "He means that we weren't *there* at that time."

Alice looked even more confused.

"But you're alive now?" she asked.

"Yes, and we were then as well, just not at that particular time," said Will.

"What Will is trying to say is that we were *sometime* else – we were travelling through time," said the Doctor.

"Well why didn't he say that?" she asked crossly.

"Hmmm. Will never uses one word where a whole phrase will do instead. One day, he'll be a very great writer – he's actually really rather good with words, you just need to hunt for their meanings sometimes!"

"But what are we going to do?" said Alice.

"I think we need the help of a detective, don't you Will?" said the Doctor.

"Indefatigably," came the reply, "And not just any detective I'll wager."

"Elementarily, my dear Will," said the Doctor laughing. Then turning towards Alice he said: "I told you he was good with words. Now, have you had breakfast yet?"

Alice shook her head.

"Then let's get us to a bakery," he said. And with that, he put a five pound note on the table to pay for the tea and they got up and left.

Chapter 17

Had it worked, Valeria wondered?

She didn't feel very different, but then she always felt the same anyway, so that wasn't going to help. But had anything changed?

She walked across the book lined room, her 5 inch black heels click clacking across the floor as she went, every footstep causing a little puff of dust to rise up from the floor, and sat down at the large carved mahogany desk that she used for work.

She drummed her blood red nails on the leather desktop wondering whether or not to pick up the old fashioned Bakelite telephone. But who would she call? Surely if something had changed, someone would have called her to let her know.

The phone had not rung.

Her brother was still sat in the red leather armchair across the room by the ornate stone fireplace, and he still wasn't talking.

Nothing had changed. Something had gone wrong.

And the room still needed a good clean.

Chapter 18

Just off to the left of the Market Square in Wizard's Thatch you'll find the most marvellous bakers and patisserie in the world and it's called 'Wood's of Wizard's Thatch' and was granted a Royal warrant by Queen Victoria who was rather partial to their sponges. Apparently, she had a habit of getting a bit peckish between lunchtime and her very late dinner, and began requesting that a tray of tea with sweet bread and butter be served to her around four o' clock to ward off the hunger pangs. Victoria sandwiches, or sponges, were soon all the rage, and eventually became the measuring stick by which all baking was judged.

Wood's has been there for literally hundreds of years and is still in the hands of the same family who have been baking in the town since it was first settled in the 800's – in fact legend has it that it was one of the Wood sisters who gave shelter to King Alfred when he first fled to the Somerset levels. It was this sister, who unaware of his identity, left him to watch some cakes that she had left cooking on the fire. Preoccupied with the problems of his kingdom, Alfred accidentally let the cakes burn.

The current master baker in the Wood family who holds the unofficial title of Royal Sponge Maker is an extremely competent chef called Ken. He trained with culinary masters in the art of baking in both Paris and London before returning to run the family business many years ago. Although getting on a bit, he shows no signs of slowing down or retiring and still gets up at 4 o'clock in the morning to ensure that the townsfolk have hot fresh and crusty bread in the mornings for their toast.

Wood's Bakery has been there so long that the rest of the street was built around it and the area was originally known as Baker's Street – although this was later shortened to Baker Street, and Wood's is at number 221.

"We're going to seek some help from a very good friend of mine," said the Doctor to Alice as they headed towards Baker Street. "His name is Shylock, and he's the world's foremost Insulting Detective. We need his help to explain what's going on."

Alice thought she must have misheard – had he really said *Insulting Detective?*

"Here we are," said Will as they arrived at Wood's of Wizard's Thatch.

"But it's a bakers," said Alice.

"Yes it is, I said we were going to a bakery - but we're not actually going in there. We're going to the apartment upstairs," explained the Doctor, "it's owned by Dr Jeroboam Watson."

"Dr Watson?" asked Alice, "I thought you said his name was Shylock?"

"I did," said the Doctor mysteriously.

"Right, now where's the door?" They were staring at the front of the building and there didn't appear to be a door to the apartment upstairs.

"Will?" asked the Doctor, "I think we need to draw on your skills… "

"No problem," said Will. Will approached the front of the building and went up to the wall besides the shop front. Taking a piece of charcoal from his doublet he roughly drew the shape of a panelled door with a doorbell beside it and wrote the number 221B at the top.

Alice wondered what on earth he was doing, but as he stepped away the strangest thing happened. Will's drawing gradually turned into a real door with a lantern hanging above it.

"How…?" began Alice.

The Doctor touched the side of his nose and said "Magic!" Then turning back to Will he said: "A short tug, if you please, Will."

Will gave the doorbell a short sharp tug and somewhere in the distance Alice could hear a bell ringing.

"Better do it again, Will – if Jeroboam is at home he won't hear it," said the Doctor.

Will tugged the bell again.

After what seemed like ages they could hear footsteps shuffling towards the door. Then they heard a muttered curse followed by an "Ooops!" and what sounded like a heavy key being dropped on the floor. A few moments later they heard the key scrape in the lock and the door was very slowly opened to reveal a slightly portly old man with white whiskers and a monocle. He was wearing an old fashioned tweed suit.

"Hello, Watson," said the Doctor. "Is Shylock in?"

"Eh?" came the reply.

"Is ... He ... In ...?" bellowed Will.

"Can't hear you, you'd better come in and see Shylock," said Jeroboam.

"He's a trifle deaf," explained Will to Alice

"I heard that, young Master Shakespeare," said Jeroboam. "Don't be so rude!" And with that, he stepped aside and allowed them to enter.

The hallway was surprisingly well proportioned and seemed to spread in all directions. There was a rather grand staircase that rose up to the first floor from a black and white tiled floor and there were palm trees and statues all around the walls. As Jeroboam closed the door, Alice noticed that there were large windows on either side – windows that weren't there on the outside she was certain.

"You know your way, I suppose," said Jeroboam as he locked the door behind them. As he walked away from the door it gradually disappeared.

Alice looked at the Doctor.

Once again he touched the side of his nose in a knowing way: "Magic!" he said again.

They all trooped up the wide and sweeping staircase to the first floor where they were met by a rather grand pair of mahogany doors. These opened as they approached, as if by unseen hands and they walked through into the private lair of the world's greatest Insulting Detective, Shylock Holmes.

Alice could not believe her eyes – the room was enormous and the windows looked down into the street outside, and yet it was at the back of the house, how was that possible? And just how could the apartment be so big? It was most definitely bigger on the inside than on the outside. In fact she was having a hard time understanding just how this building could fit beside, above, or behind the bakery that was in Baker Street.

And then she stopped as a thought occurred to her.

Didn't the rooms at home seem rather too big for the building as well? What was it her mother had said when they first went look at the house?

"Unbelievably spacious and airy for such an old building," or something like that. Alice began to think that there was a lot more to the buildings in Wizard's Thatch than met the eye!

"Aaaah!" said a voice from that appeared to be coming from the inside of a rather comfy looking, oversized (and overstuffed) armchair by the fireplace, "You must be Alice!"

She was about to ask who had said that and how he could possibly know who she was, when she realised that it wasn't the first time that that had happened to her.

Everywhere she went people knew her name.

A tall and incredibly thin man with a hook nose and long dark hair hanging around his face, a bit like a pair of curtains, unfolded himself from the armchair and stood up. He put his hand out to shake hers in a formal greeting.

"I'm so please to meet you," he continued, "the whole town is talking about you."

"Really," said Alice, "Why?"

"Because of who you are, silly," retorted Will – before Shylock could say another word. The doctor just glared at his friend to stop him from saying anything else.

"Alice has had a trying night," he explained to Shylock. "The, err, prophecy was invoked I believe," he added mysteriously.

"I don't understand," said Alice, by now getting extremely fed up with all of the goings on and the mysterious half conversations that were being held around her. "And why because of who I am?" she demanded.

"You will understand, but not yet. When…. " began Will.

"Don't you dare say when I'm older!" shouted Alice. "I've moved to a strange town, met really strange people, everyone knows my name and my father tried to murder me – what's going on?" Alice was beginning to get hysterical.

"Calm down, my dear," said Shylock firmly. "And sit down!"

Alice sat.

"I know you think that everyone is talking in riddles and that you're worried about your mother and father," said the Doctor, "it's just that we've been waiting for you to arrive for so long that we understand far more than it appears. And we keep forgetting that you don't."

"Is this a dream?" Alice asked quietly, a sob escaping through her trembling lips "Is that why this doesn't make sense?"

"No," replied the Doctor sadly, "if anything it's a nightmare. My nightmare," he added.

"But how can I be having your nightmare?" she asked.

"If only it were that simple," he replied. "Let's just say that we're all stuck in my nightmare. It began over 100 years ago and it's still going on."

"Look, sit back and let me explain," he added. "Breakfast, I think I promised you." And with that he took out a magic wand from inside his jacket and vaguely waved it towards the fireplace.

A leather footstool appeared out of nowhere and settled by Alice's feet, followed by a table that was set for breakfast. The fireplace then started smoking and a blazing fire appeared in the grate.

"One of the perks of being a wizard," explained Will.

Now, Alice had just had a cup of tea at Beattie's before they came to Baker Street, but she helped herself out of politeness really. Will added a spoonful of sugar and said "It'll help – honestly." And then he smiled at her and settled back into another armchair opposite her with a cup of tea and a toasted crumpet that was dripping with butter.

Shylock and the Doctor stood in front of the fire with their backs to it and began to explain.

"We were all there," began Shylock. Alice looked up at him expectantly, her tea momentarily forgotten, so he continued.

"Yes, you heard me rightly. All those years ago, we were all there."

Alice looked at the Doctor and Will for confirmation.

"Well, not strictly all of us," said Will. "The Doctor and I were else-when, at the time as I explained earlier."

"Else-when?" asked Alice quietly.

"That's right," said the Doctor, "Some-time else."

"If I might be allowed to continue," interrupted Shylock irritably and Alice began to realise why he was called the insulting Detective; he was really quite abrupt.

"I meant, of course, the rest of us were there, you…." Alice could see that he was on the point of insulting Will when he looked at her and thought better of it.

Will grinned at Alice. He'd obviously interrupted on purpose, she decided, to try and get a rise out of Shylock and it had worked really rather well.

"Look," said Alice, helping herself to a large slice of toast covered in strawberry jam and butter, "will someone please explain to me what on earth is going on?"

"When the Rules Britannia were strengthened all those years ago," continued Shylock, "something went terribly wrong. When they were still alive, Ezekiel, Valeria's brother, and Valeria herself were plotting to seize control of the Empire."

"They were very powerful warlocks," added Will.

"Sorry," said Alice, dropping her toast "Did you say when they were alive?"

"Yes, he did," said the Doctor.

"You mean they're dead?" asked Alice incredulously.

"It's not that simple," said Will.

"It never is," added Alice.

"They're more, err, Un-Dead really…" continued Will.

Alice sat back with a look of pure disbelief on her face, and rescued her toast that had miraculously landed jam and butter side up.

"And what's a warlock?" she demanded.

"We'd better finish our tale and explain…." said the Doctor. "Warlocks are witches and wizards who have gone over to the darkside – that have gone bad you might say. And, Valeria and Ezekiel had gone bad"

"In their case," interrupted Shylock, "extremely bad."

"I knew it," thought Alice.

Shylock continued.

"When the Rules Britannia were being redrawn in 1877, Valeria and her brother realised that it would be the perfect opportunity to 'tweak' the Rules and gain an awful lot of power. They realised that not only could they seize control of Queen Victoria's throne, but also the entire British Empire.

For one split second at the stroke of midnight, when the great enchantment was being wrought, if they could time their own magical workings just right, they would be able to wrest the power of the Rules away from the Governing Council of Twelve and seize control – giving them unimaginable power and wealth."

"Will and I had been called away," said the Doctor. "We'd received a message from Francis who was having a spot of trouble with the Spanish and needed a bit of magical help."

"So off we went," said Will. "We set off to go and help Francis else-when."

"Only he didn't need us, he had everything in hand," said the Doctor, "it was all a ruse to get us away from Bombay Manor and the Council."

Shylock continued the story: "I had discovered the ruse but only after they'd already left to go else-when. I went to see Thaddeus' younger brother, Joseph, to see if he knew a way of contacting him and bringing him back, but he didn't. He told me that Thaddeus' place on the Council was being taken that night by his sister Artemisia...."

"So you went to see her," asked Alice, helping herself to another slice of toast.

"I did," continued Shylock, "and between us, Joseph, Artemisia, Annalisa and me, we decided to come up with a plan to foil Valeria and Ezekiel at great personal expense… …"

Chapter 19

The story was once again taken up by the Doctor:

"As soon as we arrived in 1588, we went straight to Plymouth to find my cousin, Francis. He was of course on the Hoe, overlooking the English Channel, playing bowls as you'd expect him to be doing when the Spanish were threatening to invade! He also said that he had everything in hand, as they wouldn't succeed because of the Rules – so what was the hurry?"

In fact, it hadn't been quite as simple as that.

Will and the Doctor had arrived in sixteenth century Plymouth to witness one of the strangest sights imaginable: Sir Francis Drake, the Doctor's cousin, and his crew were indeed playing bowls on Plymouth Hoe – or to be slightly more precise between fifteen and twenty feet above it. On Broomsticks. Using mallets. And they were being cheered on by an enthusiastic group of spectators who were loving what they were watching.

"Ahoy there Doctor," called Sir Francis from atop his broomstick, "I've invented a new sport – and I'm going to call it Extreme Croquet!"

At that very moment he needed to duck as a croquet ball had been wacked through the air towards his head. "Damn, it's dangerous!" he muttered.

In sixteenth century England, Queen Elizabeth I had been crowned Enchantress of the Isles and the whole country was in awe of her. She was guided and advised by a group of shadowy figures called the 'School of Night' and they were rumoured to include vampires, daemons and wizards, and magic was everywhere you looked. So watching the Queens favourite pirate flying around on a broomstick in Plymouth was nothing terribly out of the ordinary.

It was only after her nephew, King James I, came to the throne when she died that magic started to go into hiding.

The score of the match was being kept by three old sisters from Ennis Moor who only had one eye between them – meaning that they quite literally turned a blind eye to fouls, misdeeds and downright cheating. It also meant that they were extremely biased in favour of whoever looked after them best.

As Sir Francis was a complete and notorious flirt, and extremely generous, his team was winning by a rather large margin.

Will and the Doctor were cheered to see Sir Francis in such good spirits and also to discover that nothing was truly amiss, so, knowing that Artemisia had everything in hand at Bombay Manor, they decided to stay a while and cheer his team on.

When the game finally ended, with Sir Francis' team 100 points ahead, the Doctor and Will agreed to help them celebrate by joining them all for a meal in a local tavern.

"Deer for my dears!" shouted Sir Francis to the landlord, demanding roast venison and gesturing to his team and his guests.

"Typical! Enjoying yourselves when it was all going wrong here" interrupted Shylock, passing another cup of tea to Alice. "But why *did* you agree to stay?"

"It was a mistake to stay," agreed the Doctor, "but you have to appreciate that I didn't know that anything was amiss at home."

"You're not kidding when you say it was a mistake," added Will, rubbing his stomach "there's only so much venison a boy can take!"

"It's not the first time you've taken venison either is it Will?" said Shylock knowingly. Will blushed.

"Look, don't get side tracked, I need to know what happened next?" pleaded Alice.

"Well, while Will and the Doctor were in Plymouth," said Shylock, "We were planning how to rescue the situation that we were facing......

"In fact the planning hadn't really been that complicated. There was no way of contacting the Doctor as he was in a time before telegraphs and he wasn't anywhere near Matilda."

Alice found herself wondering again who this 'Matilda' was and resolved to ask at the earliest opportunity.

"The Doctor, of course was in the tavern enjoying himself with that no good pirate cousin of his," continued Shylock, "whilst the rest of us were meeting at Joseph's House to try and work out what to do. Joseph quickly took charge.

He demonstrated that the only way to prevent Valeria taking control of the codicil was for a separate spell working to be cast at the same time as the codicil was being wrought by the Council of Twelve.

If they could just counter Valeria's spell weaving with a spell of their own, then all would not be lost – but what could they possibly do? Annalisa had an idea, but she wouldn't say anything in front of Artemisia.

"We'll create a diversion," she had said to Artemisia, "you don't need to know what it is in case it goes wrong. You can then deny any knowledge of it. All you'll have to do is to make sure that as the clock strikes for the twelfth and final time, Valeria must not be a part of the circle of power."

"I'll do what I can," said Artemisia, "but if we break the circle before midnight something terrible might happen."

"At least it will stop Valeria," said Joseph.

"But at what cost?" Shylock had wondered.

"We'll have to cross that bridge when we come to it," replied Joseph.

"Indeed we will," said Shylock. "Little did I know exactly what that would entail just a few short hours later….

Artemisia glanced at the clock and making her excuses, prepared to leave the house to return to Bombay Manor where the final preparations for the codicil were under way. She didn't dare to be late and didn't want Valeria to notice her absence – she didn't trust Valeria as far as she could throw her, and neither did anyone else. We all felt it would be better to keep an eye on Valeria if at all possible.

When Artemisia had gone, we all turned to Annalisa to find out what she was planning.

"You're not going to like it," she had said. Annalisa sat down, looked at her husband and myself and said, "I think you'd better sit down. You're not going to like my idea one bit, but it's the only way I can think of to stop her……" "

...

"Meanwhile, Sir Francis was in great spirits," said Will. "He had raised a glass or two to his cousin the Doctor, and of course the Doctor had to return the compliment."

" 'To Time Travel!' He had said," said the Doctor to Will, "And you countered with 'To extreme croquet!' if my memory serves me correctly!"

Will laughed. Everyone had cheered and the atmosphere in the tavern was beginning to get rowdy.

"I said we ought to be going to you," said Will, "that you should be there when the Rules were strengthened with the codicil."

"Artemisia had it covered, I thought at the time," said the Doctor, "What could possibly go wrong?"

"Where Valeria was concerned almost anything," muttered Shylock..

"I agreed, albeit reluctantly," said the Doctor, "with Will –
so thanking Sir Francis for his hospitality and promising to
look into the game of Extreme Croquet when I got home,
to see if it had survived the centuries, we bid them all a
fond farewell as the clock started to strike twelve."

...

"Else when," continued Shylock, "at Bombay Manor the
Council of Twelve were just finishing the great
enchantment of the codicil that would strengthen the Rules
Britannia for another hundred years.

The twelve most senior witches and wizards, representing
the twelve great Wizarding families, were gathered in a
circle in the Great Hall. The clock struck for the second,
third and fourth time.

"As we will," they chanted. It struck a fifth and then sixth
time.

"So mote it be." It struck a seventh and eighth time.

"Merry did we meet." The ninth and tenth strikes echoed
through the hall.

"And merry we shall part!" The clock struck for the
eleventh time, but before it could strike for the twelfth and
final time to seal the enchantment of the codicil, three
white mice covered in blood ran across the middle of the
circle.

Artemisia screamed. She was terrified of mice and she let
go of the hands of the witches to either side as she moved

her hands towards her face in horror, breaking the circle in the process.

There was a loud clap of thunder, Valeria screamed and dropped to the floor in a dead faint, the life apparently deserting her body and the clock struck for the twelfth and final time.

There was a bright white flash and then everything went silent. Artemisia and the three mice had completely disappeared. The ten remaining members of the Council of Twelve that were still standing, looked slowly at each other for what seemed like an eternity. Then Arabella Morris let out a shuddering sob and the spell was broken.

Something was wrong. Very, very wrong. The Manor was completely silent. Not only had Artemisia disappeared, but so had every other member of the Bombay family household that was outside the circle of protection.

The Council quickly organised a search party to check out what had happened. Four pairs of wizards set off to search the Manor and its grounds while the other two remained behind, keeping an eye on Valeria who was still out cold.

"At least she's still here though," said Arabella, holding back another sob. "Not like poor Artemisia. Who's g... g.. gone." She burst into tears and was comforted by her sister Maleficent.

Gradually the search party returned with strange stories about what they'd found around the building: the kitchens were completely empty, but the pans were still bubbling on the stove and the meat was still roasting over the fire; the cribs in the nursery were empty – although they were still rocking – and the mobiles above them were still turning; and even Great Aunt Aphluenza's rocking chair was still moving but there was no sign of her anywhere.

In fact there was no sign of anybody, everyone had disappeared. There were no signs of a struggle, no scorch marks to indicate that something untoward had happened, nothing at all. They just weren't there.

...

"Well, that's not strictly true," interrupted Will, "it's not so much that they weren't there – more that they weren't then...."

"I was coming to that," said Shylock, sounding quite cross that he had been interrupted mid flow. "Now where was I?"

"Not where, When!" interrupted Will, again. Shylock shot him an ugly glance.

"Oh do get on with it," said Alice, "I want to know what happened next!"

Shylock picked up the story where he had left off.

...

The ten Council members looked at each other.

"What on earth happened?" cried Arabella.

"I just don't know," replied Jedediah Tangle, the most senior member of the Council still there.

"But where are they?" Maleficent asked, "They can't just have vanished. Can they?"

It was at that precise moment that Valeria groaned, and Arabella screamed because they'd all forgotten about her lying on the floor. She was coming too. The Council members all rallied around her as she opened her eyes.

"Wh… what happened?" Valeria asked a bit shakily.

Jedediah began to explain.

"What do you mean, they've gone?" demanded Valeria, who was obviously feeling a lot better as her imperious manner was returning. "Gone where?"

"We don't know," explained Mr Burke the Chemyst, "They've just disappeared."

"All of them?" cried Valeria, "the whole family?"

"The whole family," replied Jedediah. "But that's not all."

Everyone in the room turned to look at him.

"There's something else?" asked Maleficent, incredulously.

"You mean no-one else has noticed?" asked Jedediah.

"I have," said Dr Jekyll. "It's the clocks – they've all stopped."

"And my pocket watch," added William Hare.

"Mine too," said Mr Burke.

"It would appear," continued Jedediah, "that time has stopped."

...

"And that is what happened, more or less," said the Doctor.

"But what really happened, you haven't explained?" asked Alice.

Shylock took up the story once again:

"Joseph and Annalisa were what we call AniMagi – it means they could turn into animals using magic," he explained. "Specifically they could turn into mice. White mice. As could their thirteen year old daughter Alice – it was a family trait. Annalisa knew that the only way that Valeria could be stopped was if she broke the circle, and she had decided that the best way to make that happen was for them to startle her and then, as mice, run up her cloak."

"So they turned themselves into mice," said Alice, "but where did the blood come from?"

"The only way they could get from their house," said the Doctor, "to Bombay Manor was by using blood magic. One single drop of their blood would take them to another member of the family who was in mortal peril."

"Just one drop of Joseph's blood was all it needed," said Will, "and there they were in the Great Hall of Bombay Manor, running across the floor. But towards Artemisia not Valeria. That was their mistake."

"And Artemisia was terrified of mice," cried Alice.

"Exactly," said the Doctor. "As Artemisia broke the circle they all paid the ultimate sacrifice. The protection that the circle afforded the twelve great families had been broken and the Bombay family were left unprotected."

"And every living member of the family disappeared," said Will. "No-one ever knew what became of them, or where or when they had disappeared to."

"But how did you escape? How did you survive?" asked Alice.

"Will and I were else-when. We weren't alive at the time the circle was broken," replied the Doctor, "We were still in the sixteenth century."

"And what happened to Joseph, Annalisa and the other Alice?" she asked.

"As they were members of the family," responded Shylock, "they were affected by the enchantment and the breaking of the spell, and they disappeared too."

"But not Valeria?" asked Alice.

"No," replied Will. "She was being firmly held by the Wizards on either side of her when the spell was broken so she was still being protected by the codicil. The curse that she had meant to invoke had rebounded on her and killed her where she stood."

"So she died?" cried Alice.

"So she died," said Will. "sort of."

Alice looked aghast at Will, then at Shylock and then at the Doctor. They all looked grim, but the Doctor looked grimmest of all.

"I've been searching for a way to break the curse and looking for my family ever since," he said.

Shylock coughed and cleared his throat: "Err, there's something I've always wondered." He asked the Doctor.

"Which is?" replied the Doctor.

"I thought that the Great Council represented the twelve great Wizarding families," Shylock continued.

"It does," said the Doctor.

"So why," continued Shylock, "were there two members of the Bombay family in the circle."

"That's right," said Will, thinking about it, "Artemisia took your place – so whose place was Valeria taking?"

"Her own," said the Doctor quietly.

"Her own? But how?" the others all cried out.

"Valeria was only a member of the family by marriage," explained the Doctor. "She was in fact the last remaining member of the Stanton wizards from Somerset."

"But how could she be?" asked Alice, "What about her brother Ezekiel?"

"He was already dead," said Will softly, "The Stanton's had been a very powerful Wizarding family that had lived in Somerset for generations. But over the years, different generations had gradually died out leaving just Valeria and her brother Ezekiel."

"And then Ezekiel died." said Shylock. "Valeria vowed revenge on the Doctor for not helping save her brother's life and gradually she became rather.. well, unhinged."

"Of course," he continued, "After the panic had died down at Bombay Manor and Valeria had fully come to and was back to her imperious and impossible self; no-one noticed that she no longer had a pulse and that she had in fact become 'un-dead'. As the apparent sole surviving member of the Bombay family she took over the running of the Estate."

"She vowed to get even," said Will, "that she would never cease to try and recreate the circumstances of her death in order to enforce the curse that had rebounded on her and seize control as she had originally planned."

"And that's where I came in," said Alice quietly.

"Well," said the Doctor, "and this is only conjecture mind you, we think that she engineered the whole situation with regard to you, Joe and Anna to make sure you celebrated your thirteenth birthday in the house, just like the original Alice."

"And that if she could bewitch your family to attack each other," said Will, "and make you afraid of each other rather than be the happy and close knit family that you are, then it would invoke the magic that she cast all those years ago and enforce the curse that backfired. It might even have given her the power to bring her brother back to life."

"But it didn't work," said Alice, "because I ran away."

"Because you ran away," said Will. "You're the girl who ran away."

"But why me?" Alice wondered.

"Well, that's more simple than you might think," said the Doctor, "you see, you and I are related."

Silence descended on the room in Baker Street as everyone turned to look at him with questioning looks on their faces. Everyone that was, except Shylock Holmes.

"Related?" asked Alice, breaking the silence. "But I did my family tree at school last term and there's no-one called Bombay in it – I would've remembered. I'm sure there wasn't!"

"Aah, but there was," replied the Doctor. As the others started to protest that that was quite impossible, he held up his hand for silence.

"Do you remember Shylock telling you about Joseph and Annalisa Bombay?"

"Yes, but…." Alice started to tell him that she knew all about them from the book that she had been given by Jedediah Tangle when a though occurred to her. "Hang on, didn't you say Jedediah Tangle was there? And Mr Burke, and Dr Jekyll?"

"Time really had stopped," continued the Doctor, "at least here in Wizard's Thatch it had; and it still has. The world has moved on, but everyone that was here then is still here now."

"But how is that possible?" asked Will.

"Magic," said Shylock. "Dark and terrible magic that went completely awry."

"Valeria Bombay," said Will quietly.

"Exactly," said Shylock.

"But you said that we were related?" Alice said to the Doctor. "How?"

"Joseph and Annalisa were married," he replied.

"Well obviously," retorted Alice.

"Let me finish," said the Doctor. "As I said, Joseph and Annalisa were married."

Alice looked like she was going to interrupt again, but Will placed a hand on her arm to stop her.

"Which of course means that Annalisa was a Bombay by marriage," he continued, "her maiden name was..."

"Owens," whispered Alice. "That's right isn't it?"

The Doctor nodded.

"And that's my name."

"That's right," said the Doctor. "Her maiden name before she was married was Annalisa Owens. And she was your Great Aunt, several times removed."

Alice sat there, stunned and completely lost for words.

"We thought that when you and your family returned it would help the curse to be revoked," explained Shylock, "So I, err, persuaded you and your father to re-enact the actions of that fateful night."

"What do you mean, persuaded?" demanded Alice.

"Well, sort of hypnotised really," explained Shylock.

"But you didn't ask permission," said Will, "or tell anyone else about it! How could you?"

"It was better that no-one knew in case it didn't work," said Shylock.

"It didn't," said Will, huffily.

"No," said the Doctor, quietly, "It didn't. You really should have told someone what you were up to, Shylock!"

Shylock nodded, his face lost in thoughts.

"So has it really all been a dream?" wondered Alice, "how curious."

"Much more of a nightmare really," replied the Doctor.

"And are my parents alright, then?" she asked.

"Yes, they are," he replied.

"So it's it all over then?" she added.

"For now," said Will. "Let's get you home to your family," he continued, "they will have experienced some awful dreams and they'll be waking up soon. You really should be there, or they'll be worried."

"Besides," said the Doctor, "tomorrow is your first day at your new school and I'm sure you've got things to do."

Alice nodded, unsure of whether she was glad to be leaving this strange room full of strange people.

"I've got a question," she said as she turned to leave. "Are you all wizards?"

Will, Shylock and the Doctor nodded gravely. And then they smiled.

"What did you expect?" asked Will, "After all, the town is called Wizard's Thatch."

They said goodbye to Shylock and walked down the grand staircase to the hallway on the ground floor of Shylock's apartment. Jeroboam was waiting for them and holding the door to the street open. Alice thanked him and he winked at her in a conspiratorially sort of way before closing the door behind them.

As they started to walk away Alice turned round, but the door to 221B Baker Street had disappeared and had been replaced by a small stretch of wall beside Wood's Bakery.

They were all quiet and lost in their own thoughts as they left Baker Street and started the walk back towards Regent Street and Alice's house. Around them the town of Wizard's Thatch was just beginning to wake up to the new day. It was still early on Sunday morning.

"Is the curse broken?" Alice asked as they reached her front door.

"Yes," replied the Doctor, "but the breaking of the curse is only the beginning.…"

Chapter 20

Alice yawned.

The last few days had been extremely odd and incredibly tiring, but at least she still had one day to go before her first day at school.

Every time they moved it was the same. She was always the new girl and always the one without friends who got picked on. But this time would be different she thought to herself as she climbed the stairs towards her bedroom and a well-deserved sleep. This time she knew stuff.

She opened the door and walked into her bedroom, not bothering to stifle another great big yawn – she didn't think that she'd ever been that tired before – and she crawled into bed and was asleep before her head hit the pillow.

...

CLANG CLANG CLANG CLANG

Alice woke up with a start and automatically put her hand out to silence the offending noise. It was only her alarm clock – she'd forgotten to turn it off when she went to bed just a few minutes earlier.

She opened her eyes groggily and decided that it was far too early to get up on her last day of freedom before going to school – besides after last night's adventures she wanted to spend some time with her parents.

She was about to close her eyes and turn over to go back to sleep when her eyes snapped open. Something was different.

Alice sat upright rubbing the sleep out of her eyes.

That couldn't be right.

There in front of her on the bed was a beautifully wrapped parcel, with a note slipped under the ribbon. She pulled the note out to read it.

Thank you, love the Doctor.

That was all it said – nothing more.

Alice looked at the clock. She really had been in bed for just a few minutes, but she was wide awake now. She carefully unwrapped the small parcel and then the layers of tissue paper inside.

There in the middle was a lovely old fashioned photo frame with a picture inside. The picture was the one that she'd rescued – or was it?

Alice was sure that something about it was different. But what was it?

And then she realised.

Her aunt was smiling. And that wasn't possible, was it?

There was a light tap at the door, and then it creaked open.

"Morning, sleepyhead," said her father.

"Morning," replied Alice stifling a yawn.

"Still tired?"

"You wouldn't believe me if I told you," explained Alice.

"No, I suppose I wouldn't," he said, "C'mon though, Mum's doing a special breakfast as it's your last day before you start your new school."

"See you downstairs in a minute," she said.

"Okay."

Joe left the room shaking his head. Teenagers, he thought to himself, will I ever understand them? As he started walking down the stairs to the Kitchen, he tried to remember the nightmare that he'd had during the night.

Something to do with wizards and a curse, was it? And there was a knife, definitely a knife, like the one in the shop downstairs. There was something else as well, but he couldn't quite remember what it was. All he knew was that when he woke up he had to check on Alice as he had dreamed that there was something wrong.

Clearly it had been a nightmare because Alice was her normal self.

By the time he'd had all these thoughts he was padding into the kitchen where Anna was cooking breakfast.

"I thought we'd have a traditional English," she said as she turned the bacon that was frying in the great big iron pan. It smelt lovely.

"Lovely," said Joe.

"Are you alright, dear? His wife asked. "That nightmare still bothering you?"

"Not really," he replied distractedly, "I can't really remember it, to be honest."

Alice walked in.

"Morning, mum."

"Morning dear. Do you want your eggs fried or scrambled?."

"Scrambled!" Alice and her father replied together and then they burst out laughing.

...

After breakfast, the whole family set off to explore the town.

They headed down Regent Street into the Market Square past Tatling and Twaddle's and Tangled Words Bookshop before turning left into Baker Street.

"Where are we going, dad?" asked Alice.

"You'll see," he said mysteriously.

They kept walking, past Old Slaughters Coffee House and stooped outside Wood's Bakery. Alice looked around nervously – she'd been here not that long ago and she wondered if her father knew.

"There it is," he said.

Alice looked at the wall beside Wood's, but there was nothing there.

"No, on the other side of the street. Look!"

Alice turned, and there on the corner of Baker Street and Horizont Alley was the strangest looking building she had ever seen.

"What is it?" asked Alice.

"It's the town museum," replied her father.

"It's weird," she said.

"Actually it is, but not how you think." Her father was pointing to a sign over what looked like the main entrance. It said "Welcome to the Wyrd Museum"

"What does 'Wyrd' mean?" asked Alice

"Well, according to the dictionary it's an Anglo Saxon word for karma, fate or personal destiny."

"You mean it's a museum of Karma?" asked Alice, now thoroughly confused.

"No, it's a museum of destiny – you know, fortune telling."

"Great," thought Alice, "After last night that's just what I need!"

Alice and her father crossed the road, leaving her mother on the other side.

"I'm getting some shopping from that supermarket in the Square," she explained. "I'll catch up with you after you've had your fun in the museum at the coffee shop just up the road."

Joe and Alice went up to the ticket booth.

"One and a half, please." He asked the attendant.

Two tickets were issued and in they went, up a steep stone staircase to the main exhibition hall – this was not what Alice had wanted to do, but she was in for a pleasant surprise. It wasn't a boring old museum at all, but a collection of old seaside fortune telling machines.

There were so many and they were all different. Some were quite simple and others so elaborate they looked incredibly valuable. But there in the centre was something quite remarkable.

"Look at this one," said her father, leading her towards the centre of the room.

It was quite simply the grandest thing that Alice had ever seen. A tall black box with curved glass windows and inlaid silver. It looked Arabian or something she thought.

It was set on a large square of red carpet, with palm trees around it and separated from everything else by red ropes on brass poles.

"May I introduce you to Madam Fortune," said her father in his best theatrical voice, "She's an automaton."

Inside the really ornate box was what looked like an old fashioned Victorian fortune teller – and yet there was something strangely familiar about the face.

"Do you recognise her?" asked Joe.

"Recognise her? No. Well, sort of," replied Alice, "she looks familiar."

"Here, read the story," said Joe pointing to an ornate plaque to the side of the display. Alice gasped as she began to read:

The seventh daughter of a seventh daughter, Valeria Bombay was born into this world at the stroke of midnight on All Hallows Eve in the year 1856. The secret love child of a Transylvanian count and an Irish maidservant named Megan, she was quickly taken from her mother and swept away by her aunt, a travelling Gypsy called Bella Donna.

As part of the Victorian freak show 'The World Famous Travelling Imagiscarium' which was winding its way through Europe, Bella Donna read tealeaves and told fortunes for those who were of an inquisitive mind, and who crossed her palm with silver!

As Valeria grew up accompanying he infamous aunt wherever she went, her own gift of second sight developed. Voices whispered softly to her in the night, and the pictures on her aunt's faded tarot cards—which had once meant nothing to her—began to become clear......

One moonlit evening, after the show had finished, and Valeria was undertaking her usual menial task of collecting discarded show tickets from the mud, a cloaked stranger who had been observing her from afar approached and held out his hand. A gigantic ruby ring, as red as blood, glinted in the clear night sky upon his finger.

As he stretched out his hand and pointed towards her he said with a booming voice....

"I am the messenger of the Sultan Bhardoum-al-Karir, a great and powerful sorcerer from the far off lands of Arabia, and you are chosen to be his Prophetess and Seer."

She looked at him, frankly incredulous. "Are you sure?" she asked tremulously.

"No! I am Sir Tayne of Arabia and the Sultan never makes mistakes," came the booming reply.

And so, before the night was out, Valeria was gone, whisked away by a handsome stranger on the back if his mighty black steed and holding on for dear life.

Upon her arrival in his kingdom, the Sultan named her "Daughter of the Midnight Hour" because of her jet black hair, and bestowed upon her all the trappings of an Arabian Seer. Valeria's powers grew ever stronger....

Each evening she would be summoned to the Sultan's chamber where he would cast questions written on the finest parchment into the fire of foresight and ask her to stare into a sapphire crystal orb called the Eye of Radiance.

For a time she was content, saving her gifts from the Sultan in a secret purse, but after a few years she became restless. A vision in the eye one night showed her that the Sultan's powers lay not in knowledge, but in the possession of the Eye of Radiance (which had a trapped desert djinn spirit inside) and that if she stole the Eye of Radiance then fame and fortune were hers for the taking.

The Eye also told her that her destiny lay back in Blighty, in the great metropolitan city of London, in the service of the Great Queen and Empress of the Isles, Victoria.

Valeria made her plans and set her sights on that and a career on the west end stage, where mediums were performing to packed audiences in theatres every night. She wanted a piece of the action and was determined to have it.

In October 1888, a tall woman of bohemian appearance stood at a newsstand on the corner of Drury Lane in London. She was staring at a newspaper headline daubed across a placard which read "Strange Disappearance Of Arabian Sultan — Investigation Yields No Clues".

Behind her, above the entrance to the Theatre of the Black Arts, a name shone brightly in lights: "Madame Fortune — Psychic to the Sultan — Live Tonight". The woman turned away, smiled to herself, and walked into the darkened theatre.

Little did she know that it was to be the same night that she would meet her first husband, the powerful and very rich, Ezekiel Bombay who had travelled from his estates here in Somerset, with the aim of taking her back with him that same night.

He would not be disappointed. This fortune teller is a lifelike representation of Madam Fortune before she was married to Ezekiel Bombay.

"But, is that….?"

"No, of course not" said her father. That would make her over 100 years old, wouldn't it?"

"Well she does look old," said Alice.

"Really!" exclaimed her father. "It's her grandmother I think, or maybe her great grandmother. You can see the resemblance though."

Alice knew better. The Valeria Bombay that she had met looked exactly like the fortune teller, because it was the same person. But why was her father showing her this.

"You know, it's quite strange," said Joe thoughtfully. It doesn't matter where you stand, it really looks like her eyes are following you."

Alice looked back at Madam Fortune as her father started to walk away. Alice gasped again as she was sure that she'd seen the automaton lick its lips, slightly. And it had definitely blinked.

Alice backed away. Her eyes never leaving the automaton that now looked decidedly hungry she thought.

Chapter 21

Alice's mum was waiting for them when they arrived at Old Slaughters Coffee Shop.

"Are you okay dear?" she asked

Alice mumbled a reply and sat down at the table.

"I've already ordered," said her mum, "hope that's ok?"

"She had a bit of a start," said Joe "I thought it would be fun, but I think the Madam Fortune exhibit spooked her a bit."

"It didn't spook me dad," said Alice, "it's just that it looked so real." And hungry she thought, but she didn't say that bit out loud.

"Don't you think that it's just a bit odd that the Madam Fortune exhibit looks exactly like the woman who runs Bombay Manor Estates and keeps giving us things?"

"Not really," said her father, "after all, you look just like your granny."

"Ha! Ha!" retorted Alice.

"Look stop bickering you two," said Anna. "The drinks are on their way and I thought we might head up to the castle or down to the beach perhaps?"

"Mum, its November – don't you think it's a bit cold to go to the beach?"

"Well, someone certainly got out of bed the wrong side this morning didn't they?" said Joe.

"Leave her alone Joe," said Anna, "It's all been a bit much and she's probably nervous about starting her new school tomorrow."

"I am here you know," interrupted Alice.

"I know you are dear," said her mum, "but there's nothing to worry about. I mean it's just starting a new school – it's not like anything terrible is going to happen is it?"

Alice just turned and stared at her parents. They had absolutely no idea what was going on at all.

"Interesting place this," said Joe, looking at the walls. "What's it called again?"

"Old Slaughters Coffee Shop," said Anna.

"It sounds a bit gruesome. And just what is that supposed to be?" Alice pointed at a display case on the wall close to where they were sitting.

"It's one of the original bottles of Cream's Elixir," said the man who had just brought the drinks to the table. "All of the displays belong to my family. They're all the original belongings that Dr Thomas Cream brought with him when he arrived in 1892."

"Wow!" said Joe. "Has the coffee shop been open that long?"

"Oh yes," said their waiter. "Dr Cream arrived here in November and opened the coffee shop just a few weeks later. It's been here ever since."

"Are you related to him?" asked Anna.

"You could say that," said their waiter. "My name's Tom, Tom Cream, but all my friends call me Jack." He finished laying the drinks out on the table and left them to it.

"He looks just like the man in that newspaper cutting," said Anna thoughtfully. "Maybe it's his grandfather or something."

By this stage, Alice was getting more and more scared. Could her parents not see what was going on? All the businesses in town were owned by the same people that owned them in the late 1800's. And they were definitely the same people not just family members that looked similar.

It was then that a thought struck her.

What was it that Shylock had said earlier this morning? He had said that Jedediah Tangle was at Bombay Manor all those years ago when the curse backfired. Could that have been the same man that gave her the book for her birthday as well?

There was only one way to find out. She would have to ask the Doctor. But how could she get in touch with him? He'd been there when she needed him before, but how had she managed to attract his attention?

She'd been frightened, that was it, and she felt all alone.

That wasn't going to help this time, because she no longer felt frightened. Spooked perhaps, but certainly not frightened and she wasn't alone.

She absentmindedly stirred her coffee while she was lost in her thoughts and when she moved her hand away, the spoon continued to stir the coffee all on its own.

Her parents beamed at her. Maybe she was settling in after all.

Appendix

A Guide To Wizard's Thatch

Wizard's Thatch Halt Train Station

Every journey to Wizard's Thatch begins with a stop at Wizard's Thatch Halt, the local train station. Of course, you could visit the town by car if you were able to navigate the confusing narrow lanes and the signs that appear to point in every direction apart from the one in which you want to go - so to be honest, it probably is far easier just to catch a train. That is, unless the town wants you to find it, in which case the directions are very simple and it takes next to no time at all to get there....

Tickets are of course freely available from all main railway ticket agencies - although once you are in possession of a ticket it is somewhat harder to find the platform that the trains leave from. It is said that the Great Wizarding Railway deliberately alters its timetable to discourage tourists.

Witchrose Supermarket

Witchrose is the Wizard's Thatch supermarket and delicatessen. Over the years, the locals have successfully fought off forays by all the major supermarket chains believing that independence is best. That and the sure knowledge that every little might help, but that the big four are unlikely to ever stock the local delicacy of truffle wrapped wild boar sausages at a price that they can afford.

Tangled Words Book & Map Shop

Despite the fact that tourists are actively discouraged from visiting and spoiling this gem of the English countryside, Tangled Words does sell a wide range of maps and guides to the local area including a wide range of local history books written by the locals themselves.

Tangled Words also has its own printing press and publishes the town newspaper, often referred to as "the Panic Post" - usually because there's always a panic to get it ready in time for publication. The Post (to give it its real name) is a weekly publication full of news and local interest stories. The stars are written by a local horologist and soothsayer called Madame Pumphrey who also does a nice turn in knitted tea cosies that look just like pumpkins.

It is also the main distribution point for Official Decrees and Proclamations from the Real Ministry of Magic in London.

Auntie Emm's Little Sweet Shoppe

Quite possibly the most popular little shop in the entire town. Most of the children from the Wizard's Thatch Academy spend their weekly stipend here treating Auntie Emm's as a glorified tuck shop. Emmentaal Maracas, the proprietor, makes all her own confectionery and insists that the recipes are a closely guarded family secret. Her best-selling sweets include Jelly Troll Bogies, Two Ton Tongue Ticklers and the obligatory favourites Fizzing Whizz Bangs

Burke & Hare's Apothecary

The two Williams (William Burke and William Hare) came to Wizard's Thatch in 1829 shortly after their namesakes were hung for murder in Edinburgh. Although there was much consternation upon their arrival, as they appeared to be of what was locally referred to as a rough element, they quickly established themselves as friends to the elderly and infirm, often nursing them through their final hours. Widely respected as purveyors of homemade herbal concoctions that could cure everything from whooping cough to infestations by rodents their business benefited from their elderly benefactors who often left them all of their worldly goods upon their death, simply for being there at the end. The business is currently run by their grandsons, also both called William.

Bashir's Carpets of Distinction

There are very few independent specialist carpet retailers left in England and Ali Bashir is one of the best. All of his carpets are sourced from the Bazaars of the Middle East and feel truly magical underfoot, no mass produced Axminsters here - these are carpets with a twist! Some people swear that it feels as though you're walking on air when you walk on a Bashir's carpet. Others of course know the truth... Ali Bashir serves a particularly potent mint tea to all of his customers; in fact it's surprising that they don't think they're flying.....

The World Famous Wand Emporium

Oliver van de Bombay has been making wands and staffs longer than any other retailer on the High Street. With the advent of mass production of replica resin wands in the far east, as official movie souvenirs, many traditional wand makers went out of business (the movie industry has a lot to be blamed for....) and consequently the skills required started to die out. The van de Bombay family, on the other hand, continue to hand make all of them the old fashioned way in the family workshops in Wizard's Thatch.

Aunt Beattie's Victorian Pantry

Every market town needs a tearoom, and Aunt Beattie's Victorian Pantry is one of the best. All the cakes are baked on the premises fresh each day and the cream horns have won awards, in fact Beattie's nephew Kenny (an internationally famous radio and television star from the 1950's) says he likes nothing more than one of her cream horns every morning.

Beattie's (as it is locally known) is one of a kind, and nothing is ever too much trouble for her or her team of enthusiastic staff. If you happen to be passing stop by and visit her upper floors, as according to rumour she has the best tarts in the business!

The Enchanted Manor

The Enchanted Manor in Wizard's Thatch is home to one of the most unusual museums you can possibly imagine, and is packed to the rafters with curious displays, puzzles, winding corridors and peculiar rooms. Owned and run by Dr Thaddeus Bombay, the Enchanted Manor is also home to his collection of confiscated Dark Magic Artefacts.

The Collection, as it is often referred, is housed on the first floor and is added to on a continual basis. No-one really knows how or where Dr Bombay manages to source the items, but there is no doubt that the collection includes some very unusual items indeed.

It is said that some of the confiscated artefacts are so dangerous that he never puts them on display in case someone tries to use their dark magic for their own gains

Bob Black & Quentin Decker, Ironmongers to the crown

Every town needs traditional Ironmongers, selling 4 inch nails, fork handles and hose, it's just that this one also sells cauldrons. It has to be said that most of the non-magical folk in Wizard's Thatch believe they are sold as decorative and ironic flower pots (the town being called Wizard's Thatch and all) but people in the know, know the truth..... After all, all the best spells and potions are brewed in a cauldron aren't they?

Both Bob and Quentin hire themselves out for any kind of handyman work available in the area, and are often seen squiring some of the more well do locals at gala evenings before going home with them to lag their pipes or fix their plumbing.

Wizard's Thatch Academy

One of the top public schools in the country, Wizard's Thatch Academy is right up there with Eton, Harrow, Alleyns and Winchester as one of the most sought after educational establishments for those in the know. Of course, it does differ in one major area from the others. In addition to turning out incredibly well educated and responsible members of the community, Wizard's Thatch Academy also teaches magic......

Mrs Beeton's Golden Broomstick Tavern

In addition to being a micro-brewery, the Golden Broomstick stocks a wide range of beverages including the local specialities of Spiced Pumpkin Juice (squeezed from locally grown pumpkins) and Wizard's Thatch Original Recipe ButterBeer.

Brewed to the same recipe since early Victorian times, Wizard's Thatch Original Recipe ButterBeer has been a local favourite for many, many years as both an alcoholic punch and a refreshing soft drink. The recipe was given to local philanthropist Dr Thaddeus Bombay by Mrs Isabella Beeton in 1861. It tastes the same now as when she first made it. The Golden Broomstick is named in her honour.

Bombay Manor, Wizard's Thatch Halt

Bombay Manor stands a short way outside the main town of Wizard's Thatch in a small hamlet known as Wizard's Thatch Halt. The present building was erected in 1541 as a "this is not what to do" example of construction by the Wren School of architecture. However, a testament to the building techniques of the time means that it is still standing to this day, albeit slightly wonkily. Various generations have continued to add to the building with a wing here and a turret there until it now resembles something from the "Hammer House" of architecture. Now an old and slightly mouldering pile, it is still truly a sight to behold.

The ghosts of some members of the Bombay family are believed to inhabit various parts of the building giving rise to the belief locally that Bombay Manor is one of the most haunted buildings in the country....

Wizard's Thatch Post Office & Owlery

The Wizard's Thatch sub postmistress, Penny Forum, runs the Wizard's Thatch Postal Service for magical and non-magical folk alike. Some of the locals prefer to use the Royal Mail, and others prefer the far more reliable Owl Postal Service that was set up by Mrs EM Blyton for her daughters Imogen and Mary in 1840, the year that Queen Victoria regulates the service and establishes the Royal Penny Post for non magical folk.

Penny, a descendant of Mrs Blyton is at the heart of the community and likes to keep her "finger on the pulse". What that really means is that if you want to know what's going on - you ask Penny, as she loves a gossip. She is also the originator of the phrase "Penny for your thoughts...."

The Old Abbey Ruins

Every part of the British countryside has ruins of some kind - and there are more Abbey ruins than you can shake a stick at in Somerset.

The Abbey in Wizard's Thatch was given to the Bombay family by King Henry on the strict understanding that the building was destroyed and the stones reused.

Not known for their obedience to the crown, the Bombay's tore down some of the Abbey for reuse and just left the ruins where they stood. The Abbot, a very wise man who allegedly practiced the darker arts, cursed the Bombay family for destroying the Abbey throughout the generations.

A curse that is said to exist to this very day.